PROLOGUE

*L*ovissa shook her head, trying to chase off the vestiges of dream, and heard a small squeak just left of her head.

She ignored it. The newest of her retinue was a timid young thing, but she did very well at keeping the furs and pillows of Lovissa's nest exactly as she preferred them. Regina would be embarrassed enough at her squeaks, and might well remove herself from the ranks of those who served the queen if Lovissa were to notice.

Instead, she stretched her short front legs out and let an arch ripple down her spine, coaxing old, tired muscles into alertness. Her dreams had been restless. No visions, and she knew herself to be growing impatient with their absence.

It would take five to save dragonkind, and only one had come. Surely the Dragon Star would not make them wait too long for the next.

Lovissa harrumphed and pushed to her feet, dragging herself the short distance to the cave opening. It was arrogance itself to presume she knew the intentions of any star, and surely one who *hung in the skies for time eternal had learned more patience than any dragon queen.*

She breathed in the air of a morning that held far too much promise of spring. Already, Baraken reported snowmelt in the lower passes. It would not be much longer before the elves poured through, seeking vengeance. The dragons had won the last battle of fall, and that would not have sat well around their clan hearths in the winter. It would be the most foolish elves who came through the passes first—those who did not yet know enough to value the skin on their feet and the wisdom of their elders. But foolish elves could be just as dangerous as wiser ones, especially if the new arrow fletchings had also spread from hearth to hearth.

The fletchings had taken down Eleret.

Dragonkillers.

Lovissa knew she wasn't the only one who smelled the coming of spring. Early though it was, Baraken had already gathered the young dragons down below. The newest in the warrior ranks, and those most likely to be foolish. Wisely, he was giving them far too much to do to be imagining flights of solo glory through the northern passes.

Lovissa let her nostrils huff her amusement. The last dragon to take such a flight had been Baraken himself. It was good that he was keeping those who would seek to be foolish heroes busy. They would lose dragons in the battles of spring, of that she was sure, but she preferred to lose them only when absolutely necessary. Let the elves freeze the skin off their feet. Her dragons would stay warm and dry and practice the tactics that would keep them alive.

She winced as two youngsters diving sharply off a low ledge crashed into each other instead of the ground. Baraken was

DRAGON KIN

LILY & OCEANA

SHAE GEARY
AUDREY FAYE

FIREWEED PUBLISHING

COPYRIGHT

Copyright © 2017 Shae Geary & Audrey Faye

www.audreyfayewrites.com

working on landings, the kind a dragon with a dozen arrows in their wings might need to make. The kind that might drop them safely under the next flight of arrows—or land them at an angle where their fire could wreak vengeance.

Especially if foolish elves trapped themselves in narrow mountain passes.

Lovissa sighed. Her appetite for battle had been larger once. Too many dragons were dead, and her dreams were no longer haunted only by their ghosts. She saw, far too often for her comfort, the ones who would come. The brave dragons who no longer needed to be warriors—and the ones who rode on their backs.

Mortal enemies become kin.

She had tossed and turned all winter over such memories. And kept them to herself. The elves who would be in the passes come snowmelt did not seek a dragon to ride. They sought a dragon to kill. She would not make it easy for them.

Lovissa huffed out another breath into the early morning light and lifted her wings. She had never flown skies filled with dragonkiller arrows, but in her day, she had been the finest single-wing flyer in the Veld. She would go help Baraken train the youngsters.

And perhaps keep them alive a little longer.

PART I
A CALLING

CHAPTER 1

*L*ily craned her neck and sighed as the road reached the top of the latest rolling hill. Still no sign of River's Bend, and if the town didn't show up soon, she was going to die of dust inhalation. She glared at Alonia. "Why did your cousin have to decide to marry a farmer, anyhow?"

Alonia just snorted and rolled her eyes. "We have a whole week away from chores and lessons, and you're complaining?"

"Yes, she is." Kellen grinned, skipping over the top of the hill like it was nothing. "I think we'll be there soon."

Kellen had been saying that since the crack of dawn, and it was almost lunchtime. Lily eyed the dusty road ahead and the smaller tracks joining it from the left. That was a good sign. Most roads converged on a town eventually, so the more of them that joined together, the better the chances that they weren't horribly lost.

And a town called River's Bend better have something other than dust to welcome them.

"Here." Sapphire held out a canteen, amused sympathy in her eyes. "Pour a little water on your face and get happier or you'll scare all the wedding guests away."

Even Lily had to grin at that. "If Lotus were here, that could have been her job."

Sapphire didn't say anything—she just took the canteen back and quietly capped it.

Missing her dragon. Lily felt bad for saying anything, but she'd wanted her friend to know that she wasn't the only one thinking about a certain peach-pink menace. One who had been left safely behind under Afran and Kis's watchful eyes, because taking a teenage dragon to the biggest wedding in ten midwinters would have been the absolute height of folly.

It was going to be a huge occasion. Four days of parties and ceremonies and all the food they could eat. Alonia's cousin was marrying a really rich farmer.

The food part sounded the best. Inga's cooking was fine, but it was good, solid peasant fare. Lily's clan had been full of spice merchants and traders, and even if she'd been a lowly orphan, the scraps that landed on her plate had still tasted of stories and excitement and lands far away.

Inga would probably fall over if anyone tried to add exotic spices to her stews. Or Inga could quit, which would be even worse. Peasant food was infinitely better than food Lily had to cook for herself. She patted the last of the breakfast roll she'd tucked into her tunic. Kellen had packed their journey food, but they were down to nuts and berries and a few squirreled-away leftovers, and a rich farmer's wedding was going to put those to shame.

Lily sped up on her way down the hill. It couldn't be that much further.

Kellen joined her, matching her short legs to Lily's longer strides. "You must be hungry."

Lily didn't bother answering—or looking back for the other two. Alonia had probably stopped to pick flowers for her hair again. She wanted to look pretty when they arrived, just in case her cousin had any cute, eligible male relatives. Which was going to be the biggest headache of the next four days. "How do you suppose we keep Alonia from running off with the first elf who kisses her and promises to make her happy?"

Kellen grinned. "We don't."

"Karis expects us to keep her out of trouble." And woe to the elf who ignored their teacher when she spoke in that particular tone of voice.

"Karis knows exactly who Alonia is, and if she wanted us to keep her away from boys, she would have sent Irin along." Kellen seemed totally unconcerned that they might head back to the dragon kin village without their curvy, dreamy friend. "She'll come back because she wants a dragon."

Lily snorted. "As much as she wants a boy?"

"I think so," Kellen said quietly.

Lily wasn't nearly so certain, but any thoughts she had on that subject were interrupted as they arrived at the crest of the next hill. The view over this one was of far more than dust, a deeply welcome vista of neatly tilled fields with green crops and stone fences and comfortable cottages stretching as far as the eye could see. Her eyes widened as she spied a much larger house than the others.

"That's one of the manors," Alonia said cheerfully, weaving tiny yellow flowers into her hair. "Not one of the really rich ones, though. Those are closer to town."

Sapphire scanned the view. "Where are your clan lands?"

Alonia waved a vague hand. "Out the other side of town and into the forest. But don't worry, we won't be going there."

Lily rolled her eyes. They already knew that. Not enough boys. Most of Alonia's clan would be in River's Bend anyway, ready to celebrate and eat a rich farmer's food for four days. A rich *human* farmer. Which was just weird. Most elf clans stayed well away from human habitation. Trade was one thing. Chasing eligible boys without elf ears was a totally different matter, even if they were cute.

Sapphire eyed a dark strip of trees over to the left. "Maybe we can camp in the forest."

That would make Lily happier, but she was very sure Alonia wouldn't be on board with that plan. Especially since their fearless leader was already headed down the hill at the fastest pace she'd set for the whole journey, shaking her head. "No. My sister's letter said they would have a whole city of tents set up for the wedding guests, with bedding and free food and hair ribbons and everything."

Lily didn't bother arguing—there was no way they were going to win out against hair ribbons. She kept her eyes on the forest, though. It seemed like a lot of trees. Human farmers usually cut down every tree they could to clear more farmland. "Why is the forest so big?"

"Because of the floods." Alonia was nearly running, speaking around short, puffy breaths. "The river gets wild in the spring. It didn't used to, but then one year back when my great-grandmother was a girl, it flooded almost the whole valley, and a lot of the really nice manor houses got ruined."

Rivers didn't do that for no reason. "Why did the river change?"

Alonia shrugged and pulled an apple out of her tunic. "The farmers say there's a demon in the mountains. One of the really old elves in my clan said an incredibly big pile of stones fell and blocked one of the other arms of the river, so now all the snowmelt comes down this one."

The farmers were foolish to believe there was a demon, especially if there was a really big pile of rocks upriver somewhere. "We could camp by the river. It's not spring."

Alonia took a fierce bite of her apple. "I'm camping in the field with everyone else who's coming to this wedding, and you're sharing my tent, so stop arguing."

Lily had rolled up in a blanket to sleep more times than she could count, but someone had to keep Alonia from making all the boys trip over their own two feet for the next four days. Most men, even the not-so-young ones, took one look at her ample curves and rosy cheeks and golden curls and promptly forgot how to walk in a straight line.

Alonia stopped suddenly, and Kellen nearly ran into her back. Then they were all staring down at the new vista that had opened up in front of them—and this time, it was more than hills and farmland. The town of River's Bend in all its majesty, stretched out in a wide, haphazard circle. Lily could see at least four roads leading to two gates with sentries in what looked like red uniforms, although they were far enough away that it was hard to tell. Maybe red was just a popular color here. Shacks and small buildings made up the town proper, but around them, streaming in every direction, was a forest of tents of every shape and color. Some were sleeping tents, ranging from small ones to ones large enough to hold an entire village. Some were flimsy awnings covering a table of market fare. Lily hoped some of those were the promised food. The last bites of two-day-old meat pie in her tunic suddenly sounded very unappetizing.

She looked over at Alonia, who was practically glowing—and hadn't moved her feet since she'd spied the town. "Come on, silly. If you stand here gaping all day, all the tents will be full."

"I don't need a tent." Alonia skipped down the road arm in arm with Kellen. "I just need a place to change my dress and a sweet boy to bring me something cool to drink."

Lily ignored the last part—there were no boys in sight yet. She eyed Alonia's simple dress, made of the same fabric as her tunic and leggings. "What's wrong with your dress?"

"Nothing, if I were feeding dragons or carrying firewood."

Dragons didn't care what people looked like. Irin said so, and his face was living proof. "You're supposed to save your best dress for the wedding."

Alonia skipped backwards, giggling. "You think I only brought one?"

Lily looked at Kellen with a raised eyebrow.

Kellen just laughed and willingly skipped in circles with Alonia. "I only brought one, but I'm not looking for a boy. I'm waiting for a dragon."

Kellen had been waiting longer than anyone. It made Lily's heart hurt sometimes. She wanted a dragon too, but she didn't expect one to pick her. She didn't like fire—too hot and prickly—and they all knew it. She was the misfit of the dragon kin village. Which was fine with her—it was a lot better than being a clan orphan, even in a clan with really good food.

"She's not sad today," Sapphire said quietly, her eyes on their smaller friend. "We shouldn't be sad either. She's not going to find a dragon at a wedding, so we should help her find all the other good things."

Keep Kellen distracted until a dragon finally got smart and picked her. That was a plan Lily could get behind. "Fine. I'll do that. You get a good, strong piece of rope and tie Alonia to a tree somewhere so that we can find her when it's time to go home again."

Sapphire laughed. "She'd just get rescued by six handsome boys."

Not if the tree was deep enough in the forest, but Alonia probably wouldn't cooperate with that plan. Lily sighed and adjusted the straps of the rucksack on her shoulders.

It was going to be a long four days.

CHAPTER 2

*L*ily turned sideways, squeezing between tightly pressed dancers who didn't seem to care who they squished. An errant sleeve caught on the swirls of her burnished copper armband, and she barely resisted the urge to stab its owner with the matching copper branches of her headpiece. She'd somehow let Alonia talk her into wearing her clan festive wear for the first night of dancing. Which was reasonable—many of the elves she could see had done the same, but most of their clans didn't adorn themselves in headwear designed to mimic a crown of branches.

She loved the elegant bands of copper wrapping her head, and Alonia had braided it on tightly enough that she could probably go swimming with it, but it had been attracting attention all night. Or her dress was. She wasn't the only elf there with bare shoulders, but clearly farmers tended to keep themselves more covered up.

Which was foolish. It was hot, even this late in the day,

and most of the farm girls had gone from having rosy cheeks to seriously sweaty ones.

Lily kept squeezing between dancers. She finally got to the edge of the packed field and took a deep breath of air that didn't smell like sweaty farmer. The sun was just tucking down into the horizon, beginning to paint its oranges and reds across the western sky. Bedtime for the daylight, but not for those gathered for the wedding. The revelry would go on for hours yet.

They'd eaten under the bright sun of the late afternoon and then the music had started, and the dancing. First the small children, pulling people up to dance with them, and then the ones of an age to find themselves a partner for the night—or longer. The groom's human kin had been eyeing the elves in attendance with avid curiosity, which had expanded Alonia's suitors exponentially and tempted Lily to go into early hiding. She wasn't the only one. Sapphire was probably up a tree by now, and Kellen was small enough that she could pretend to be a child when she wanted to.

Lily ducked into the first, beckoning trees, and let the cooler air brush her cheeks. The river lay this way, and her skin and throat were begging for water.

She slowed her walk, moving off anything that looked like an obvious trail and melting into the shadows of some of the taller trees. She had no interest in advertising her presence.

She'd never been a friendly elf.

After a short, cool walk, the trees thinned again and she could see the sparkle of the river, hear its quiet gurgle. Here, close to town, it was a well-mannered and lazy flow, although Lily could see evidence of its springtime antics. She picked a small dip where the bank got lower and knelt down by the water, doing her best to keep her dress out of the damp dirt. Not that it mattered much—even if she went back to the crush of bodies on the field, nobody was going to be looking at the hem of her skirt.

She trailed her fingers in the water, letting the cool soothe her, drain away some of her temper. It wasn't Alonia's fault that big crowds were annoying, and it was nice to be away from the village for a while. Lily just needed to do it on her own terms. Ones that didn't involve too many people trying to step on her feet.

She lifted wet fingers and trailed them over her cheeks. One drop ran down to her chin and plopped off, trailing down inside her dress and making her laugh. Oh, to be a little girl again, one who waded into the river, dress and all, any time she chose. She cupped a little of the water and stuck her tongue in it. Tasting. Water that drifted too close to human lands sometimes tasted foul, but this was upriver of the town, and the drops on her tongue were cool and sweet. Perfectly safe for an elf to drink, and a lot cooler than most of the fruity punches arrayed on tables around the dancing.

She cupped more water, using both hands this time, and drank, careful not to let too much of it dribble down her chin. The fields weren't as dusty as the roads, but this many feet had still kicked up some, and she didn't want to be the embarrassing elf with a stain of mud running down her front. She owed Alonia that much effort.

Two more handfuls of water and the parched feeling in her throat finally began to ebb. They'd shaken the dust of the journey off their clothing, but she'd had far too much of it still riding inside her. She gave the river another sad look—it was perfect for swimming. Just deep enough, and with a gentle, swirly flow that would play with her hair if she floated on her back to watch the sunset.

She let her fingers play at the water's edge instead. That would have to do.

The ripples teased her fingers, calling to her, and then it wasn't the water and the sunset she was seeing anymore—or not only those. A picture formed over top. A painting. One that moved and looked very real, just as she might see through her own eyes. But this wasn't the view through her eyes. And wherever it was, it wasn't here.

Lily blinked, hard, but nothing changed.

She could see a building, or part of one, with columns of stone and a doorway that curved like the roof of a rondo. There was water, but not this water. Not the kind that flowed over rocks in a burbling stream. Dank, dark water, the kind that sat and grew smelly things, sometimes even dangerous things.

Lily felt her nose wrinkling, even though she smelled nothing. The elves of her clan would work to fix the water, to drain it or move whatever obstacles were impeding the water's proper flow. Here, in this awake dreaming, she could do nothing.

She heard a small whiffle, almost like a cat. Whoever's dream she shared was tired. Weary, and not just for a night's sleep. Their bones felt heavy, like one who had lived a very long time and no longer had the strength to stand.

Lily blinked again, trying to get whatever weird vision

had seized her head to go away. She didn't want the dreams of some stray cat or visions of sick water she couldn't fix. She wanted a drink and some peace, and a magical dose of patience to survive the next four days without killing Alonia or some overly hopeful farmer.

The dream wavered a moment—and then Lily saw the claw. The one covered in tiny, shimmering blue scales that caught the last rays of the sun. Translucent skin stretched between the claws, tinged with that same, shimmering blue with touches of gray and green.

Lily moved her head, trying to see more. She knew what that claw was—anyone would who lived in a village of dragons. A tail flicked into view, covered in scales that were undulating blue-green jewels. Lily wanted so very badly to touch. To see the face of the dragon who wore water in all its most beautiful colors. Who, even now, curled up to sleep on the edge of the dark waters, chin resting on its jeweled tail.

Lily gasped. She was seeing as the dragon saw. That wasn't possible. She lifted her fingers out of the water, scrubbing her eyes, and the vision vanished. She shook her head, moving it left to right, trying to bring back the beautiful tail. Nothing. Gone, as if she'd imagined it.

She scrubbed her eyes again, more frantically this time, reaching out in her mind for the dream of the blue-green dragon.

Nothing.

She heard a small, sad whimper and realized she was the one who made it.

She made a face and wrapped her arms around herself, her fingers falling over her copper armbands. She should be imagining a soft bed with a pillow of goose down to pull over her head and block out the noise. Daydreaming of dragons was a clear sign of too much fruit punch. No dragon would come this close to humans, and no dragon would need to work this hard to find Lily. All they had to do was fly into the dragon kin village on any day besides this one.

She sighed and cupped her hands. One more drink and she'd try to find the tent where they were meant to sleep.

The moment her fingers scooped into the water, the picture in her mind was back. She froze, barely daring to breathe.

This time, the feelings that came with it were stronger. Sleepy dragon, but not the easy weight of welcomed sleep. The heaviness was nearly choking, almost as if the one falling asleep wished to never wake up.

Lily's eyes flew open in horror.

Her dragon didn't want to wake up.

Her dragon.

She leaped to her feet, urgency suddenly beating a sharp rhythm inside her chest. Then she doubled over again, stabbing her fingers into the water. "I'm coming. Don't you dare move. I'm on my way." To where, she didn't know—but she knew which way. Up the river.

She ran a half-dozen steps and then skidded to a halt, her brain finally catching up with her feet. She couldn't go alone into a strange forest at night, not without Karis stripping all her skin off her body once she got back. She needed to find her friends. All of them. Alonia because she knew these woods. Sapphire because she might have some stray milk curds in her pocket and she'd done this before. Kellen because she was really smart.

Lily's feet flew, skirting the edge of the dancers, desperately trying to catch sight of her friends. People glanced at her, eyebrows raised, but she didn't have time to stop and explain. She jumped to dodge a child who got in her way and then turned, skidding to a halt. People ignored children, but they saw everything. "Have you seen my friend Kellen? She's about this big and she has red flowers in her hair."

"I'm right here."

Lily spun around and grabbed Kellen's shoulders.

Her friend shook her head, laughing. "You're running around like a lunatic—what's going on?"

"My dragon is calling me."

Kellen's laugh died, her eyes wide.

"We have to go. Right now." Lily tugged on Kellen's arm, desperate to get moving. "Where are Alonia and Sapphire?"

"Sapphire went with one of the healers to get a new salve for Kis." Kellen scanned the dancers helplessly. "Alonia is probably in there somewhere."

They'd never find her. Not before full dark, and Lily's fingers needed to be back in the water with a fierceness she could barely contain. "Then we have to go without her."

Kellen shook her head. "She knows these woods. We need her."

A pair of blond dancers swung by and nearly ran them over. Lily grabbed the arm of the elf, who looked surprisingly like Alonia, but wasn't. Kellen darted into the crowd and came out a moment later, flushed with success. "She's coming. She just has to finish this dance."

Lily nearly screamed. "My dragon is more important than dancing."

"I know, but we need to get Sapphire anyhow." Kellen's feet were already running. "This way. I told Alonia to meet us by the river."

Lily ran, barely keeping up with her fleet-footed friend. They ran around the dancers and into a neat row of tents, vying for space near the excitement. The rich farmers had provided free food and drink, but there were lots of vendors here offering baubles and trinkets—shiny, pretty ones that might have tempted Lily on any other day. She looked around as they ran, her eyes frantically seeking the bundled herbs and potions of a healer.

"This way." Kellen dodged between two tents at full speed. Lily hopped over the rope lines, cursing, and nearly ran into Kellen's back.

Sapphire looked up from the bottle she was smelling, eyes wide and astonished.

"My dragon." Lily managed to get the words out before she sucked in a breath. "We need to go. She's in trouble."

Sapphire set the bottle down. "Which way? Where?"

Lily's head felt like it had gone down a waterfall in a wine barrel. "I don't know. We need to follow the river." She took one more breath and started running back the way they had come. Footfalls behind her said she wasn't alone. She didn't bother dodging dancers. She headed straight for the river and cool air and rippling water.

This time, she didn't pause on the river bank. She jumped right in—feet, hands, even her face.

She could see nothing, and her heart caught in her throat—and then she felt it. The dim, slow breaths of sleep.

Lily gasped for air and pushed everything she could at that sleeping mind.

I'm coming.

CHAPTER 3

Lily narrowly avoided face-planting into yet another tree and cursed. Quietly, because her friends were also tripping over roots and limbs and knotted fronds in the pitch-black and were ready to kill her for dragging them out on this wild goose chase.

Except it wasn't a goose they were chasing. It was a dragon, and she was still sleeping—or she had been the last time Lily had touched her fingers to the river.

"I could be dancing with Rolpho. Or Landis." Alonia picked her way through a dense batch of fronds, her voice pitched to the perfect whine. "Or Merifreet."

Lily wrinkled her nose. "What kind of name is Merifreet?"

"He's from a family of rich merchants," Alonia said primly.

They all were, at least to hear them tell it. Humans had the oddest fondness for making sure you knew just how much wealth their family had even before you started dancing. And they seemed to assume the same of hers, especially when she wore her copper branches. Lily reached up to make sure she was still wearing them—the night had already torn one of her slippers and the sleeve of Sapphire's dress.

The only comfortable one was Kellen, who had somehow arranged to be wearing her usual tunic and leggings. She was also lower to the ground, so she wasn't getting quite as badly banged and bruised as they made their way through the trees.

Sapphire sighed somewhere in the dark. "Are you sure we can't take the road? The walking would be a lot easier."

The road was too far away from the river. "I can't feel my dragon from the road."

"What kind of dragon talks in the water, anyhow?" Alonia sounded cross, but she also sounded a little bit envious.

Sapphire snorted. "Dragons aren't supposed to hatch in trees either, but that's where I found Lotus."

Getting to your dragon wasn't supposed to be the hard part. Lily bent down and untangled her foot from a particularly grabby vine. "The sun should be up soon, and then it won't be so hard to walk." She tried to move faster. The sun might also wake up her dragon. It would be a lot easier to find her if she was still sleeping.

"I don't see any buildings," Kellen said quietly.

Lily could only hope the waking dream had been a true one. "I think it was one of those manor houses Alonia told us about earlier. One that flooded." Was still flooded, with water that smelled bad and filled her dragon with sadness.

Lily shook her head, trying to rid it of the thoughts that

had been chasing her all night. First, she would find her dragon. Then she would worry about everything else. She squinted through the trees ahead, looking for a break in the darkness. There was a sliver of moon in the sky, and manor houses had clearings and fields around them, not trees and thickets. Or at least they did until they flooded.

Floods changed everything, and Alonia's great-grandmother was old. The clearings and fields would have had a long time to turn back into forest.

Lily veered toward the river again, needing to feel the connection, wavery though it was, with her sleeping dragon. The others followed her, well used to the routine by now. Kellen took a seat on a big tree root and waited patiently. Alonia fretted. "How could a dragon live in the valley like this without anyone knowing?"

Lily ignored her, fingers in the water, soaking in the quiet, whiffling slumber.

Kellen shrugged. "Maybe she only goes out at night."

"She sleeps at night," Alonia said dryly.

They could figure all that out after they got there. Lily stood up again and splashed out of the water. Her slippers were wretched messes. They were intended for dancing, not a hike through the woods. "I think we're closer."

Alonia made a face. "You said that last time."

And the time before that, and the time before that. It had been true each time.

Sapphire squinted into the dark. Lily was pretty sure she was trying to send a message to Lotus, but they were two days' travel away. Even kin bonds didn't work from that far.

"Look." Kellen pointed at the east horizon. "The sun's coming up."

The fear Lily had been hiking with all night scaled into panic. "She'll wake up. She might leave."

Kellen's hand, warm and comforting, landed on her arm. "If she does, she'll come find you. That's what dragons do. They find their kin."

Lily wasn't nearly so sure. She'd never heard about a call like this. And her dragon felt wrong. Dim somehow. Dark and sick, like the water.

Alonia sucked in a sharp breath. "There."

Lily followed the direction of the handwaving and tried to see. Alonia might only have half a brain sometimes, but she had really sharp eyes. "I don't see anything."

"I do." Alonia grabbed her fingers and started dragging.

Lily went willingly, peering into the very first wisps of light creeping through the dark. Her heart thundered in her chest, willing the manor house in her dream to be there.

"I see it too." Kellan's voice was hushed, almost reverent. "It's falling down."

Water did that, and so did houses without anyone living there to keep them strong and tidy. Lily's eyes finally spied an angled line that didn't belong to a tree, and she let go of Alonia's hand, running toward the thinning trees and the strange shadows of a half-fallen house.

She froze as her feet touched water, and looked down. They'd arrived at the edge of a dank, fetid swamp, spring flood waters held in place by the natural contours of the land and heated by the summer warmth into a stinky stew.

Alonia's nose wrinkled. "It smells worse than the stables."

It was only going to get worse as the sun came up. Lily dipped her fingers into the water, her need to sense her dragon overriding her disgust. Still sleeping, but more lightly. She peered at the ruins, trying to figure out where a dragon might be hiding. There were only a couple of parts of the house still standing that looked large enough to be the room she had seen. She gathered up the skirt of her dress and peeled off slippers she should have taken off hours ago.

"Wait." Kellen looked almost panicked. "Don't. That water's terrible."

It was, but there was no choice. "My dragon's in there somewhere. I need to find her."

Kellen looked at the dank water, confused. "No dragon would choose to sleep by water. Especially when it smells this bad."

Sapphire nodded. "Lotus wouldn't come anywhere near this. She doesn't even like getting close enough to heat the hot pool."

Lily gritted her teeth. "Maybe my dragon is weird like me. I know she's in there."

Sapphire dipped her hand toward the water and stopped before she actually touched it. "Maybe we can find a boat."

Something frantic clawed at Lily's insides. She needed to go. Now. "Farms don't have boats, and there's no time for us to build a raft or drain the water." She took her first steps into the swamp, gritting her teeth and trying not to think about what she was stepping in. "You went up a tree in the middle of the night for your dragon."

"I don't think this is a good idea." Alonia sounded like she might be sick any minute.

Lily took two steps deeper into the water. "Wait here. I'll be back as soon as I can." This wasn't theirs to do. They couldn't feel her dragon, or how heavy she was, how close she was to going to sleep for good and never waking up again. How much emptiness lived inside the most beautiful blue-green scales Lily had ever seen.

The water was getting deeper—deep enough that there was no point trying to hold up her dress. Lily let it fall into the dank wet, grateful that the sun had crept up high enough that she could at least see a little. She wasn't sure she wanted to see a lot. These waters were deep enough that swimming things likely lived here.

She jumped as something nibbled on her toes and shook her head, ashamed. Just a little fish. If her clan could see her now, they'd send her off to live with the landlubbers. She wrapped her arms around her waist and kept walking. The water wasn't getting much deeper. She headed toward the most intact part of the manor house, one that had four walls mostly left standing.

The curious fish traveled with her, and apparently, it had friends. More nibbles on her toes and legs, and not all of them were as friendly as the first one. Lily shuddered and kept going. Her dragon was inside. Unless something in the swamp had venom or really big teeth, she was going in.

She was almost to the standing wall when her feet struck something hard. Stone, flattened on top. She stepped onto the cool surface, grateful to have her toes out of the muck, and felt around. It went sideways along the standing wall. Lily looked back at her friends, who were standing at the edge of the swamp in various states of dismay, worry, and shock. She turned back to the wall. There were three windows along its length, all too high for her to climb in.

She set one hand on the wall for balance and headed to her right. There had to be a door somewhere.

The water rose higher up her legs, and she grimaced. Maybe the other way was better, away from the river, but she was almost at the end of the wall. She made her way gingerly around the corner. The stone underfoot hadn't deterred the fishes any, but at least the footing was less creepy. She kept moving forward, feeling carefully with her feet. There were more breaks in the stone over here, and a clear tilt toward the river—but this was also the side with the door. She could see the stone arching over a large opening, one that had probably been the entrance to the interior of the house when it had been intact.

More importantly, it resembled the arch she had seen through her dragon's eyes.

Lily walked faster now, caution thrown over by the stirring she could feel within. Not awake yet, but much closer. And with that stirring, a return of the weight. A dragon unhappy that morning had come.

She almost ran, not caring if she fell, rounding the edge of the arched entrance and charging in—and then nearly splashed face-first into the big pool of water flooding the whole room. She managed to get her feet back underneath her, but not before she was wet all the way up to her elbows. She cursed. She'd tripped down a set of stairs. The water was much deeper in here. She held up her arms gingerly and looked around. Three high windows let in light from the east, but it was early morning yet. She squinted into the shadows. Something as large as a dragon shouldn't be hard to find, even in the dark.

Nothing.

She'd been so sure. The room looked exactly right, but there was no sleeping dragon on a ledge, or an awake one, either. She shoved her hands into the water. Her dragon was here. Somewhere. There must be another room.

Then she heard it. The tiniest of sniffles, cut off like its owner had been startled. She spun toward the sound, coming from the darkest corner of the room.

Nothing.

Another chopped-off sniffle.

Lily walked very slowly toward the corner, her heart in her throat, looking for the shadow that would be a quietly snoring dragon. And stopped in shock when she finally saw it, curled up, head on tail, nose sniffling quietly into the dim.

Still asleep—and no bigger than a cat.

CHAPTER 4

*L*ily waded the last distance over to the ledge in the corner, an elf in a waking dream, and froze as an eye opened. She caught a flash of her bedraggled self, seen through the eye that had just opened, and then the vision vanished.

No matter. Lily could see her dragon now. Hear her short, shallow breathing.

Scared.

Lily kept her voice as quiet as a whisper. "Hello."

The spines on top of the dragon's head quivered.

"I'm Lily of the Water Healer clan, and I think you're my dragon."

That pronouncement got exactly zero reaction from the watching eye.

She had no idea what to say next. When dragons chose their kin, the bond just happened. Everyone knew that. She'd never heard of a dragon who just kept watching their kin with suspicion. She cleared

33

her throat a little, grimacing at the taste of the air. It was almost as bad as the water. "I don't know why you're in here, but this is a nasty place for a dragon to sleep."

Two eyes watched her now.

"I don't think you're a baby, because you don't feel like a baby and a baby never could have flown in here, but we need to get you out." Into the sunshine and far away from this nasty water. Lily tried to imagine what might tempt her dragon off the ledge. "Maybe we'll build a nice fire to warm you up."

A tail splashed into the water, and the real room was overlaid with a vision of the room—without Lily in it. And a decided feeling of home.

Lily blinked. "You *live* here?" That was crazy. It was a stinky, wet mess.

The tail dipped back into the water. This time, the vision moved. Tiny, deep-blue claws on this very ledge—surrounded by bits of eggshell.

Lily gaped. "You were born here?" That was crazier than leaving an egg up a tree.

The dragon settled her head back down on her tail.

The tail she had just put in the water. Lily's cold brain tried to catch up. Her dragon had just gotten wet. On purpose. And when she did, the moving pictures came. She stared at unblinking black eyes. "You talk through the water?"

A quizzical look.

Hmm. Lily put her fingers in the water, which probably wasn't necessary, since she was standing in it up to her waist. But maybe it would make sense to her dragon. This time, she didn't speak out loud. She only thought. *Can you hear me?*

Nothing.

Lily frowned. Apparently, the water only worked one way, but her dragon had seemed to understand her fine when she spoke. "Dragons hate water."

Chittering, almost like laughter. The small blue-green dragon languidly put her tail back in the water and rested her chin on her claws.

Something in Lily's throat felt too big to swallow. Her dragon was really weird. Just like her. "I like the water too. The elves of my clan like to swim and splash, and when the water is sick like this, we heal it."

Mild interest, and then one of the black eyes closed. The heaviness, coming back.

"Wait!" Lily could hear the panic in her voice and tried to tamp it down. "Show me when you were born again." There was something she needed to see.

The dragon raised her eyebrow ridges, but the picture reappeared in front of Lily's eyes. She studied it carefully. Water, just like now, but not sick water. Sunlight streamed in, and she could see that the water was clear. The stone walls didn't have water lines on them, and the hint of clearing she could see out the archway was neat and tidy and not covered in bush and bramble.

Lily could feel her sadness—and her awe. "You've lived here for a really long time."

One black eye closed again. Not interested. Curling back up into the emptiness.

"Don't go back to sleep." Lily used the voice Irin used on Lotus when she flew barrel rolls through the village.

"Are there any other dragons here? Any people? Who feeds you?"

A brief, wavery vision of a fish.

Lily felt sick. Her dragon had hatched here, maybe as far back as Alonia's great-grandmother's time. And lived with only fish for company since then. "You can't stay here. It isn't good for you." Dragons needed connection with others—it was why they had kin. And other dragons. And why everyone bugged Kis all day long.

Lonely dragons got sick in the head.

Maybe like this one. A dragon who didn't want to wake up.

Lily reached out a hand, slowly, where the black eye could see it. "I have a dragon friend named Lotus who really likes to be scratched under her chin."

Suspicion was back in the black eyes.

She needed a distraction or her finger was going to get chomped. "Do you have a name?"

Puzzlement, but less suspicion. "A name is a thing that people call you. A word that only belongs to you."

A blue-green tail swished in the water and caught the first rays of direct sunlight.

Lily stared at the shimmering scales, enthralled. "You're so beautiful, just like the colors of the ocean."

More puzzlement, and wordless curiosity this time.

Lily let her mind think of the view of the sea from the cliffs beyond the village, just in case her dragon could read her thoughts, even a little. Most dragons could. "The ocean is every shade of blue and green, and when the sun shines, it sparkles just like your scales. And it's big. Water in every direction as far as you can see."

A pink tongue snuck out and licked her finger.

Lily's heart lurched. "Would you like that for a name? Oceana?" She liked it. It sounded fancy, and the total opposite of fire.

Another lick, and the emptiness pushed away a little more.

It needed to go away completely, but that was never going to happen waist deep in stinky water or on a ledge where her dragon had slept alone for the last hundred years. This place was some kind of terrible dungeon, and she needed to break Oceana out.

She reached forward the last little bit and slid her finger under Oceana's chin. The dragon startled and then rubbed a little, just like a cat. Lily kept her motions really small. This might be the first time her dragon had ever been touched. The thought made her want to weep. "I live in a village near the ocean. It has lots of dragons, and people who make milk curds, and rondos that are nice and warm to sleep in."

Oceana seemed mostly interested in the finger scratching under her chin.

Lily's knees started to knock together from the cold. "We can't stay here. It's not safe and this water is sick, and the people around here don't know about dragons." She had no idea what they might do to one the size of a cat. Big dragons could take care of themselves, but Oceana was tiny. "I think you need to come back to my village with me."

Suspicious eyes, but Oceana didn't move her chin away.

Lily scratched like her dragon's life depended on it. "You could stay with me. Our rondo is small, and Alonia sleeps there too. She talks too much, but the dragons really like her, and she's got a good heart, even if she's a bit silly sometimes. She puts up with me when I'm cranky, and she always knows where to find the first spring berries."

A strong vision of berries on a bush, red and plump and juicy, and remembered delight.

Lily knew that bush. It grew in swamps, and the berries weren't nearly as tasty as they looked. It hurt her heart that those might be the best thing her dragon had eaten since the day she was born. "There are more kinds than that. Black ones and blue ones and shiny purple ones that are my very favorite. Kellen bakes them into pies sometimes."

A flicker of interest, but the emptiness was closing in again. Lily gulped. She didn't know how to push it back. It was too strong in this place. "Please. I need you to come with me." She reached for Oceana with two hands and picked her up, almost wanting to shake her. "We're supposed to be together. I can feel it, even if you can't, but we can't stay here."

They'd go to sleep on the ledge together and never wake up, empty and cold and surrounded by water that only knew how to help things die.

Two black eyes studied hers, and then a blue-green tail wrapped around her arm.

It was all the answer she needed.

CHAPTER 5

Lily cuddled her dragon tight to her chest and made her way across the last stretch of water to her friends. They all stared, absolutely silent, as her steps rippled the water, stirring up dank smells. Alonia's eyes were as big as stew bowls, but Sapphire and Kellen were smiling.

Lily nuzzled her chin into Oceana's spikes and carefully made her way up the muddy incline. The relief she felt stepping out of the swamp was immense—and caused instant terror in the creature on her chest. Oceana hissed like a feral cat and stabbed her claws into Lily's arms, her back spines sticking up every direction.

Lily nearly dropped her, wincing from the pain, and scrambled to hold onto her terrified dragon. "It's okay. Everything's fine. These are my friends."

Oceana gave her a baleful glare and jumped out of her arms and back into the swamp. She swam over to a half-rotted log protruding out of the murk and climbed out, shaking droplets off her back. Then she shook the water off her wings and hissed again.

Alonia took a step back, mouth gaping. "Your dragon swims?"

That didn't seem like their biggest problem at the moment. Lily grimaced and stepped back into the swamp, prepared to go tangle with a really annoyed dragon.

"Here." Kellen pulled a small wrapped package out of the pouch at her waist. "It's my fruit tart from last night."

"She's a baby," Sapphire said dubiously, eyeing the still-hissing dragon. "She needs milk curds. That will hurt her belly."

Kellen shook her head. "I don't think she's a baby. See how her spikes are darker on the tips? She's old."

Lily already knew that. She took two careful steps toward Oceana, trying to project a calm she didn't feel. Black eyes watched her balefully, but the hissing had stopped. "These are my friends. They're going to help me get you back to the village I told you about."

She heard Alonia's whispered protest, sharply cut off. There was no way they were taking a dragon to a wedding, even a really small one. Slowly, Lily unwrapped the smushed tart and broke off a small bit, holding it out on her palm. "Smell this. It tastes a whole lot better than fish."

Oceana eyed the crumbs suspiciously.

Lily kept her voice low and singsong and took another step closer. "You must be hungry. You just woke up."

A pink tongue flicked out and grabbed the tiny nibble of tart.

Lily waited. The black eyes didn't look any friendlier,

but she could feel surprise. Pleasure. "Liked that, did you?" She picked up the cloth that held the rest of the tart. "You can have the rest after we get out of this stinky pond."

Kellen gasped quietly behind her, but Lily knew what she was doing. She'd watched Irin with the baby dragons and Kis often enough. Sometimes you just had to say how things were going to be. "I'll carry you, but you need to let my friends be close by. They'll help find us food and water and places to sleep on the way home." Which was going to be roughing it, because all their packs were back at the wedding.

"I'm not sleeping in the dirt," Alonia said crossly. "I know some trails through the forest we can take to go around the town, but we'll pass close to the field on our way by. I'll go get our things."

"I'll go," Sapphire said dryly. "You'll stop to talk to a boy and we'll never see you again."

Lily started to tell them all to be quiet, and then she saw Oceana's head, tilting like she was listening. She backed up toward her friends and kept her eyes on her dragon.

"Kellen should go get our things. She'll have the least explaining to do." The rest of them were in their dance finery, and any young woman still wearing that in the morning would have many questions to answer.

Oceana was still watching.

Lily backed up the mud slope and held out the fruit tart to her friends. "Want a bite?"

Alonia looked horrified, but Kellen held back a giggle. "I could eat the whole thing right now."

A pink tongue slurped the entire tart before she

finished speaking. Oceana danced away again, her tail back in the water, and glared balefully at Kellen.

Alonia shook her head. "She's just like you, Lily. All piss and vinegar."

Scared piss and vinegar, no matter what anyone else thought. Lily bent down. "You're not going to like this next part. We'll walk along the river for as long as we can, but we need to head deeper into the forest soon, away from the water, so no one sees you."

Oceana felt puzzled.

They could explain the strange relationships of humans and elves and dragons later. "We'll try to stop by water every night, but it's going to be a dry and dusty walk." She thought about the dim dark inside the ruins. "And the sun will shine on us all day long, so you'll probably feel hot and itchy."

Oceana's tongue darted out and licked a crumb off her nose.

Kellen giggled. "She's a dragon. They like sun and dust."

Not this one. Lily knew that as well as she knew her own name. "She's not like other dragons."

Sapphire wrinkled her nose. "Can we maybe wash her off, if she doesn't mind water? She doesn't smell very good, and you don't either."

That was the best plan she'd heard in days. Lily held out her arm to Oceana. "Come on, stinky creature. Let's go play in some clean water for a bit."

Oceana didn't move. She just sent a picture again. Of her room. Of her ledge.

Lily sighed and crouched down. The swamp and ruins

didn't seem like a place anyone would want to stay, but to her dragon, they were home. "You've never gone anywhere else, have you?"

No answer, but blue-green scales shivered, even though it wasn't cold.

Lily shook her head. Great. She'd bonded with a swamp dragon. "Leaving your home isn't fun. I know that. I remember leaving mine, and I was cranky for a long time. I missed all the food I knew and my favorite hiding places and even a couple of the people who were nice to me." There hadn't been a lot of those, mostly because she hadn't been very nice back. "But the place I went was a lot better. I think you'll like it there."

Skepticism.

Lily snorted. People always tried to reason with dragons, and it never really worked. It was time to be tough again. "You can't stay here. You'll be safe in the dragon kin village."

Black eyes narrowed.

Kellen squatted down beside Lily and smiled shyly at Oceana. "There's a big oven in the kitchens there. I like making fruit tarts."

Oceana tilted her head and made a soft whirring sound.

Lily grinned. Bribery worked too. "I'll pick the berries. Now let's go to the river and get clean. They won't feed us if we smell like swamp monsters."

Oceana blinked and marched off, nose in the air, straight toward the river.

Lily followed as fast as she could move her feet. They really did smell terrible.

CHAPTER 6

*L*ily plunked down in the dust at the side of the small trail they were following and glared at her dragon. "We can't stop here. We need to get up this infernal hill and back down the other side and into the forest before somebody sees you." Which would be a lot easier if Oceana hadn't flatly refused to be carried. Zooming around in the forest was one thing, but out here, nobody was going to mistake her for a really oversized sparrow.

Oceana blew a snort at the dust on her scales and looked decidedly displeased.

"I know it's dusty. I don't like it either, but the river you want to follow doesn't go the right way."

Oceana turned herself around three times on a prickly patch of dry grass and lay down in her makeshift nest.

Alonia groaned. "This is the worst wedding ever."

They'd heard some of the wedding revelry as they'd passed by in the forest, and Kellen had seen more when

45

she'd snuck in the back way to gather their belongings.

She'd also come back with a half dozen really tasty pastries, but those were long gone.

Lily looked longingly at the water in her canteen. She wanted nothing more than to pour it over her head, but they wouldn't reach more water for hours yet. She scratched under Oceana's chin, trying to keep her crankiness at bay. She had a dragon, and that was worth eating all the dust in the world. "We can get to the spring tonight if we don't dawdle." It wasn't a river, but it had a small pool of some of the cleanest water she'd ever met. More than enough to wash all the dust off weary travelers, even the dragon variety.

They just had to survive that long—and get Oceana to move her stubborn feet. Or to let someone else move her. "No more flying. You can walk or you can ride on my rucksack."

"Don't make her mad," Sapphire said quietly. "If she breathes fire right now, we're in really big trouble."

Lily looked around at the dry grass and winced. There was a reason why the dragon kin village was basically on a hill of boulders. "If we don't get her to move, we're in really big trouble too. Ideas?"

"She already ate all the pastries."

Her friends had gamely shared most of their food, so Oceana couldn't possibly be hungry anymore.

Alonia sat down beside them and took a metal cup out of her rucksack. Lily didn't bother rolling her eyes—Alonia already knew what she thought of carrying an extra cup along when every other normal person just drank out of their canteen.

Alonia poured a stream of water into her cup and Oceana's head snapped up, swiveling toward the sound.

Lily frowned. "Are you thirsty?" They'd only left the river a little while ago, so that hadn't even occurred to her. She held out her hand, curved to hold water, but Alonia shook her head and offered her cup in the direction of Oceana's nose. "I don't mind if you drink out of my cup, beautiful."

Oceana uncurled herself and leaned her head over the cup, sniffing. Then she turned around and plunked her tail in the cup, chirring happily.

They all stared.

Lily raised an eyebrow at her dragon. "That's a little weird."

Alonia shrugged and set the cup on the ground, slowly and carefully. "She can be strange if she wants to."

Alonia might be soft-hearted enough to tolerate dusty tails in her drinking water, but Lily wasn't. "We can't exactly walk down the road this way." If they didn't get to the spring by nightfall, they were going to have far bigger problems on their hands than a cranky dragon.

Sapphire sighed and flopped back in the grass. "I keep trying to call Lotus, but she can't hear me."

"Of course she can't." Kellen poured a little of the water in her canteen down Oceana's tail and into the cup. "The village is too far away for them to hear us. We're four smart elves and one small dragon. We can figure this out."

Kellen always saw shining possibilities. Lily wished she was like that, but mostly what she saw was dust. She tried to figure out just how to walk down the road with a dragon who refused to be carried and wanted to stay wet.

She reached into the pouch at her waist and pulled out the small square of rough fabric Kellen had used to wrap the pastries. "Maybe I can make this wet and tie it around your tail."

Oceana made a sound somewhere between a hiss and a growl.

Stubborn dragon. Lily shook her head and tried to wedge the cloth into the cup beside Oceana's tail.

This time, Lily felt the growl all the way inside her. Her eyes widened as realization landed. "She's not just using the water to stay wet. She needs it to communicate with me."

Her three friends all looked at her strangely.

Lily knew she was right. "She called to me from her swamp, but it only worked when both of us were touching water. Same thing when I went into the ruin. She put her tail in the water to talk to me there."

Alonia started to giggle. "You mean we have to get back home with her tail and your fingers in a cup of water?"

Lily groaned. This was turning into one of those really bad minstrel ballads. "I'm going to have to carry her. That's the only way."

It was the only way, but by the time the sun was sliding down to the edge of the sky, Lily was beginning to regret she'd ever heard about dragons. They weren't even halfway to the spring yet. They'd had to stop too many times while one of her friends made the long trip back down to the river to fill up their canteens.

Which hadn't been at all helped by the number of times Oceana had spilled water out of the cup.

Lily tried not to be mad at her dragon. She'd lived in a

swamp her whole life—she had no idea what it meant for water to be precious. Lily sat in the shade of the large boulder they'd picked as their camping spot for the night and smiled wanly at red-faced, sweaty Kellen, who had just run all the way to the spring and back to fetch fresh water. "Thank you."

Kellen smiled quietly and stroked Oceana's cheek. "No problem. I want her to feel welcome."

Lily sighed. If Oceana had been smarter, she would have chosen Kellen as her kin, who never got frustrated and would have walked the whole way home on her knees without a word of complaint. Lily took the cold canteen Kellen offered and poured some in the dusty, dented cup.

There were a lot of new dents. Oceana was fond of flicking her tail when she was annoyed, and she'd been annoyed pretty much all day.

Alonia squatted beside them and held out two handfuls of berries, one for Kellen and Lily, and one to the dragon who was eyeing her doubtfully. "They're a little sour, but they're all I could find."

Alonia was the best of them at finding things that grew wild. And Lily wasn't picky about what washed the dust off her throat at this point. She took a couple of the berries and popped them in her mouth, squishing their meager juices around before she swallowed. She didn't mind the sour, but she came from a clan that was a lot more adventurous in their eating than most elves. She took two more berries and pushed Alonia's palm at Kellen. "Here, you eat the rest. You three have been doing all the work running to get us water."

Sapphire dropped a small bundle of twigs and sticks

down by the boulder and chuckled. "You've been lugging a dragon all day, and I remember how heavy that is. How are your arms feeling?"

Like two river reeds that had been stomped on by giants, but complaining wasn't going to fix that. "Maybe you can sit with Oceana while I set up our bedrolls." Lily made a face at Kellen. "I'd offer to cook too, but I think this day has been bad enough already."

Kellen laughed and wiped her sweaty face on her arm. "I'll cook. Alonia found us some mushrooms and wild onions, so I'll make a stew."

Alonia had been busy before they'd left the forest, scrounging up enough for a decent dinner. Lily let herself yearn for the spring and its plentiful berry bushes one last time, and then she pushed to her feet. Oceana wrapped her tail around Lily's leg and hissed at Sapphire.

Sapphire giggled and backed up, hands in the air. "How about I do the bedrolls, and you sit right there with Mistress Crankypants."

Oceana hissed again, but she seemed less riled this time.

Lily leaned down and tapped her on the nose. "If you aren't nicer to my friends, you won't be getting any of my stew."

Kellen looked at the small dragon doubtfully. "There won't be any meat in it—do you think she'll eat it?"

It was either that or subsist on dust, but Oceana hadn't exactly been swayed by reason so far. "I have no idea." Elves liked mushroom stew a lot, however, which was more than enough reason to make it. "She's not a baby dragon who needs to eat every time she breathes. Kis only eats once a day, so maybe she's like him."

Kellen raised a surprised eyebrow. "You think she's that old?"

Lily frowned. They'd already had that discussion, but maybe Kellen had been running for water. "If what she showed me is really her memories, she hatched just after the flooding happened."

Kellen's eyes got soft and sad. "Poor little girl. I bet you didn't have much company, did you?" She scratched under Oceana's chin, and to everyone's surprise, the dragon allowed it.

"It must have been so hard to have been alone for that long." Sapphire finished arranging some of the smallest twigs into a little stack and reached into her pouch for the dry bits of fluff and bark she'd gathered in the forest. Starting a fire wasn't something any of them did very often, but Irin always had a pocket full of something dry to burn, and anyone who'd ever spent more than a handful of breaths with him learned to do the same.

Sapphire reached back into her pouch for the two small rocks collected in a far-off location the dragon and kin involved refused to disclose, and tapped them together sharply. Lily exhaled gratefully as sparks immediately flew into the dry tinder. At least some part of this day was going to be easy.

Then she felt Oceana's alarm.

Lily reached for her dragon just as every spike all over her body rose straight up and blue-green wings unfurled sharply.

Sapphire jumped to put her body between Oceana and the tiny flames, but that was exactly the wrong move. A hissing ball of fury charged between her legs and a violent blue-green tail knocked Sapphire, her fire-starting rocks, and the precious pile of tinder in every possible direction.

Lily had the air entirely knocked out of her as Sapphire landed in her lap, and they both watched in stupefaction as one blue-green dragon, who suddenly looked much bigger, hulked over the baby fire's remnants and dared anyone to come closer.

Nobody moved a muscle. Four shocked faces glanced at each other without ever taking their eyes off Oceana.

A gasp, and Kellen pointed at the sky. "Look."

Lily wasn't about to do that. They were pretty sure Oceana couldn't breathe fire, but now would be a really bad time to learn they were wrong. Then she felt the air moving around her, stirring up the fire remnants and the trail dust and blowing sticky hair off her face. She still didn't look up, but she knew what the swirling wind meant.

Dragon, incoming.

It wasn't until she heard the delicate set-down that she dared to take her eyes off her dragon, and only because Oceana was staring up in absolute awe.

Another blue dragon, this one much paler, and much bigger, poked her nose down at Oceana. "Well, aren't you a tiny thing to be causing this much ruckus."

Oceana's hiss spluttered out almost as soon as it began.

Fendellen made a noise that sounded almost like a chuckle. "Feisty, too."

The dragon who would be queen after Elhen. Lily stared at the huge presence who had just landed in their dusty campsite, and couldn't find enough water in her mouth to swallow. But she also couldn't leave her dragon facing royalty alone. "Her name is Oceana, and she's my dragon."

"I know she's yours." Fendellen's voice was gentle, and a bit curious. "She's not all the way convinced of that yet, but she will be."

Something that had been tight all day loosened in Lily's chest. "Is that why the bond feels funny?"

Fendellen's huge head nodded gently. "I believe so. She has been alone a very long time. She doesn't know how to connect with anyone properly, never mind her kin."

That was awful—and it gave Lily purpose. One that made a lot more sense than dragging their feet over neverending dusty trails. "How do I help her?"

The sound that was almost a chuckle again. "Apparently, you find her some water."

Three hands promptly offered three canteens. The last of their water.

Fendellen shook her head. "She's lived in water her whole life. She needs far more than what you have with you. I've sent for Afran and Karis. They'll find a couple of unbonded dragons willing to carry riders and come collect you shortly." She blew a puff at Sapphire. "Your troublemaker is on her way too."

Rescue. Lily had never been quite so glad to hear of incoming fire-breathing monsters in her life. She winced. Her dragon had just thoroughly killed a few sparks in some tinder. She was going to throw absolute fits once she discovered flames could come out of Fendellen's mouth. "I don't think she likes fire very much."

Fendellen's tongue slid out and licked Oceana's nose. "She picked the right kin then."

The queen-to-be made it sound almost like it was meant.

Alonia gulped hard and knelt near Fendellen's head. "We don't have anything to feed you except raw mushrooms, but I have some sweet-smelling leaves in my pouch that are tasty to chew." She tipped up her head. "How are you even here?"

Fendellen blew a puff in Sapphire's direction. "This one was making an awful noise in her head, yelling for her dragon even though Lotus couldn't possibly hear."

Sapphire's eyes were big like an owl's. "But you heard me?"

"I did. It's a connection all dragon queens have with all dragon kin. Ours is perhaps stronger because of the flying lessons." Fendellen glanced over at Oceana. "Or perhaps because of how you and Lotus are connected to this one."

Lily felt her insides crumble. "Oceana isn't my dragon?"

"Of course she is." Fendellen licked the smaller dragon's nose again. "I must say, I didn't expect another of the five to show up this soon."

The rest of Lily's insides turned to dust.

Fendellen's tongue flicked over Oceana's forehead. "She is marked by the Dragon Star." Deep blue eyes turned to meet Lily's stunned gaze. "As are you."

CHAPTER 7

*E*veryone was waiting at the village outskirts. Everyone.

Expecting the new ones chosen of the Dragon Star. Which had obviously made a mistake. They couldn't even walk for a day without disaster. Lily looked at the collection of dragons and kin and villagers and turned sideways so that Oceana, finally sleeping on the back of her rucksack, wouldn't see them if she woke up. It had been a very long and weary trek, thanks to her dragon's utter refusal to climb on board any of the dragons who had come to pick them up.

Which meant none of her friends had either. They'd arrived as they'd left—four very dusty, tired elves and Lotus lurking in the distance. It was a sign of Sapphire's dragon's growing maturity that she'd backed off after a hasty series of licks and hugs. Oceana's hisses had been very clear. Fendellen was acceptable company. No one else with scales was.

The queen-to-be landed in a small whirlwind of air and dust. "Don't fret. Irin will clear them out of the way, and then we'll take Oceana straight to the nursery."

Irin was tough, but there were a *lot* of dragons in the crowd.

Lily felt, rather than heard, the amusement in her head. ::Worry not, youngling. If some should remain after Irin's efforts, they will have me to deal with.::

Afran. She could feel the relief rising inside her. Everyone listened to Afran.

::The Dragon Star has chosen. They wanted to witness your arrival. We shall give them another moment, and then the path will be cleared.::

Lily swallowed. Afran rarely mind spoke to anyone other than Karis. It somehow drove home the thought she had managed to avoid for the long, interminable day of dusty hiking.

The Dragon Star had clearly lost its mind.

"You can worry about that later too." Fendellen moved her graceful bulk to block the view of their waiting audience. "Right now, we have a dragon to get to the nursery. I know your bond hasn't settled yet, but can you wake her up?"

Their bond had so far seemed next to useless, and waking Oceana up seemed like the height of foolishness. "She'll just try to fly away again."

Fendellen rumbled, amused. "She can try."

Even Lotus had struggled to keep up with Oceana when she'd tried to flee, but the queen-to-be had calmly chased her down and herded her back to Lily, over and over. "Thank you for helping us get her back here." They'd been crazy to think four elves could do it alone.

"She will save us," Fendellen said softly. "Anything I can do to ease your journey will be done." She gazed deep into Lily's eyes. "It will not be an easy one."

The latent dread Lily had been walking with coalesced in her belly. "Because our bond is broken."

Fendellen shook her head. "Not broken. Struggling to form. She doesn't know how to open herself to another. The queen bond is weak as well."

That was news, and not of the welcome kind. "How do we fix that?"

"We've already started." Fendellen lowered her head until her nose was right next to Oceana's dreaming sniffles. "We love her, and we do our very best to understand who she is and what she will need from us."

That sounded so simple, but the last three days had been anything but. "I don't know how. I'll need your help." It was a hard admission.

"Not mine." Fendellen was already backing away. "My job is to help Afran herd the riffraff. Yours is to send gentle waking thoughts to your dragon and take her down to see Kis."

Kis was great with babies, but Oceana wasn't a baby. "What if she tries to fly away?" Kis was fierce, but he couldn't take to the skies.

"There are many fliers here who can catch her now. We'll have some keep guard until she settles."

Lily could hear the distance in Fendellen's voice. A traveler already on the road. "You're leaving?" It seemed the height of arrogance to ask a dragon of Fendellen's importance to stay, but ask she would. "Oceana knows you. She trusts you."

Fendellen blew gently in Lily's direction. "It is you she must learn to trust first. Let Irin help you with that. He knows much of dragons with wounds on the inside."

The man who ran the nursery and taught them all weapons was already stomping up the hill to meet them. It pained Lily to think of Oceana as wounded, but she had felt the darkness and the emptiness. "Will she get better?"

Fendellen launched herself skyward. ::She already is.::

"Well." Irin strode over, making no effort to be quiet. "Enough of standing around, missy. Let's get your dragon something to eat and a cup of water for her tail." He nodded at Sapphire. "Your mischief maker has been very patient. Go."

Sapphire sent Lily one last look full of friendship and worry and pride and ran toward the incoming pink-peach blot in the sky.

Irin laid a hand on Alonia's shoulder. "Karis has a bath waiting for you and a change of clothes." He gave her a dry look. "And if you wouldn't mind taking a pass through that gaggle of dragons down there, maybe you can give them something more interesting to do than watch me stomp around."

Lily almost managed a tired smile. Alonia loved flirting with the unattached dragons, and there were more gathered by the village than she'd seen together in ages.

Kellen just stood, looking uncertain.

Irin's voice got oddly gentle as he glanced her way. "Kis has been a cranky old man ever since you left, missy. He's been watching the door for two days now, waiting for you to come visit."

Kellen gulped. "I don't have any meat pies for him."

Irin snorted. "It's your heart he wants, not your excellent cooking. Go. Inga will send something over for both of you."

Lily's eyes widened as Kellen ran off, trailing dust and happiness behind her. "We're not going to the nursery?"

Irin shook his head and started walking. "Fendellen wasn't thinking. She finds her comfort there still, but from what I hear, this girl of yours isn't used to enclosed spaces or other dragons."

He'd clearly heard a lot. Lily walked alongside him, trying not to jiggle the snoring package on her back. Fendellen might think waking Oceana up was a good idea, but Lily wasn't remotely convinced. "I don't know how to help her. She's scared and she won't listen and she hasn't bonded with me properly."

"I don't know about that." Irin waved a hand to stop her protests. "Fendellen told me how the bond feels, but feelings are a luxury. What matters is actions. She came with you. She left her home and came out into the big, scary world just because you asked her to. That right there is a bond, a big and powerful one, and you would do well not to forget it."

Lily crashed to a halt and stared at him.

His lips twitched into something that might be trying to be a smile, and then he was walking again. "A bond isn't something out of a ballad. It's not meant to put quivers in your belly and stars in your eyes. It's a partnership, and those are built on actions. Choices. There is no tighter bond than the one of soldiers on the battlefield, and they never sit around and flutter their eyelashes at each other."

Lily's own lips twitched. She'd seen Alonia trying that often enough. And Irin's words, gruff as they were, soothed something inside her that had been building toward panic. "What actions will help make it stronger?"

There was approval in his glance. "We'll go to the kitchen. Inga is through for the day, and I hear your girl is fond of nice things to eat."

Food had been the only thing that had stopped Oceana's frantic flights into the sky. Afran had arrived bearing a basket of treats, and Lily had walked most of the day handing small bites up to her shoulder. Which hadn't been all that easy while constantly holding a cup of water in the vicinity of her dragon's tail. Maybe in the kitchen they could use one of Inga's old pots instead. "She'd probably like some water."

"Already set up. One of the old rain barrels." Irin's face didn't change, but his voice was tinged with amusement. "Inga's right fit to be tied, so you might stay out of her way for a bit."

A rain barrel in her kitchen. Lily could only imagine.

The snores behind her right ear were getting more sporadic. "Fendellen thought I should wake her."

Irin snorted. "She's fond of fancy entrances, that one. Me, I'm smart enough not to wake sleeping dragons, especially old and cranky ones."

His words settled some of what had been riling in Lily's belly. She fell in beside Irin as they entered the village proper. As they turned toward the large rondo that housed the village's main kitchen, she finally let herself relax a little. They were home, and mostly in one piece, and there were lots of smart people here who knew how to deal with difficult dragons.

Her relief landed just long enough to pass through the kitchen door. Then claws dug into her shoulders, a terrified hiss whirred past her ears, and a blue-green streak headed straight for the open window.

Irin got there before Oceana did, moving with a speed that astonished Lily almost as much as her dragon's antics. He shook his head at the small, hissing menace. "Oh, no you don't, missy. There will be no more of that until you have something to eat and show us that you have some manners."

Lily's eyebrows flew up at his sternness. Her dragon might not understand his words, but she clearly understood his tone. Oceana still hissed, but quietly. She backed slowly into a corner and tucked in behind Ingrid's collection of brooms.

Lily winced. Those brooms were one of the few things in the village capable of going up in flames. "I don't think she has fire, but maybe we should move her."

"She's a water dragon. She has no fire."

Lily stared as Irin crouched down to get a better view of the corner. "I never heard of a water dragon."

"Kis remembered a story. An old one that we heard in the border lands. Dragons no bigger than cats, living with noble human families and swimming in their moats." He paused. "The story we heard said there weren't any left."

Oceana chittered in the corner, very quietly.

Irin nodded his head at Lily. "Go on, then. She's yours.

Best you convince her to come out and have something to eat."

Lily wanted to hear more of the story Kis remembered, but right now, her dragon needed her. She crouched down in the dirt close to the corner. "If you're hungry, there are treats for dragons who can behave."

Oceana made a noise that sound like chirring and hissing at the same time.

Lily managed not to laugh. She knew what it was to feel grumpy and amused and not want to let go of the first. Which made her feel better. And gave her an idea, because it wasn't treats she wanted right now. It was something wet for her throat, preferably a whole bucket of it. Maybe her dragon felt the same way. She stood and backed up in the direction of the rain barrel sitting incongruously in the middle of the floor. "I'll take you down to the river later and we can have a proper swim, but this will do for a start."

She trailed her fingers in the water and watched Oceana's whole body light up. "We can get your scales all nice and shiny and clean and show everyone here just how beautiful you are."

Irin snorted quietly at her back.

She knew what he thought of Alonia's girly nature, but it didn't matter. Lily was proud of her dragon, and she wanted everyone to know it. "Come on out from behind those brooms. Those will just get you covered in more dust, and we've had enough of that for three lifetimes."

The noise Oceana made sounded almost like agreement.

Lily held out her hand, covered in dripping water.

"It's cool and it doesn't stink nearly as much as your swamp." It still wasn't anything an elf would want to drink, but for bathing, it was perfect. "I'll help you get in."

Oceana gave her a disdainful look and walked over to the barrel, nose in the air.

Lilly rolled her eyes and crouched down. "Would you like a lift into your bath, Your Royal Highness?"

Oceana hopped onto her shoulder, a move a little trickier and a lot more full of claws than when Lily had been wearing her rucksack. She winced and stood awkwardly, shifting her dragon onto the half cover on top the rain barrel. Then she put her fingers in the water and waited for Oceana's tail to join her.

She exhaled as Oceana's contentment flowed through the water. "So much better."

A chitter of disagreement, and the ruins and the dank water showed up in Lily's vision. She stared at her dragon. "You have to be kidding me. It was not better there." She crouched down and looked straight into black eyes. "Your water smelled like a herd of cattle had died there, and you didn't even want to wake up in the mornings because it was so empty and lonely and dull."

A gruff chuckle behind her. "It's certainly none of those things here."

Irin, making sure neither of them felt alone. Lily leaned into his stern, solid presence and kept being firm with the dragon who needed her to be. "You're going to take a nice swim, and then we'll go look at the treats Inga left us, because she's probably never going to let you into her kitchen again."

Oceana's eye ridges raised, and she turned her head, surveying the kitchen from one end to the other.

Lily hoped the banked fire didn't look like anything scary. There was nothing but coals and a kettle hanging over it, but the heat still coming off the coals was substantial.

Her dragon hissed a little as she spied the huge hearth.

"It's nothing." Lily scratched under a blue-scaled chin and tried to project calm. "It will be a big fire in the morning to heat the water for soup, but we'll be long gone by then." There were rain barrels all over the village. A bath outside wouldn't be nearly this warm, but maybe a dragon who'd lived her whole live in cold ruins didn't care so much about that.

She blinked as Oceana's tail flicked. Lightning quick, her dragon hopped down from the barrel and shot up a table leg. Then she marched regally right along the table's edge, surveying the cutting boards and plates with every possible treat to tempt a dragon and her kin.

Lily flew toward the table to stop the inevitable bad manners, but Irin grabbed her arm before she'd taken two steps. "Let her be, missy. She's just surveying her domain. Getting used to the place, just like a cat."

Lily blinked. She'd met a few cats, but never spent enough time with one to know their habits. But Irin appeared to be right. Oceana hadn't attacked the plates—in fact, she was almost ignoring them. Dark blue claws walked right to the end of the table and took a hop to a stool near the fire. Lily winced. They'd all spent most of a day picking tinder out of their hair after the last fire her dragon had met.

"She might not like fire, but cats like it warm." Irin had let go of Lily's arm, but his eyes were still on the dragon who was circling on the stool, tilting her head at the hearth. "Maybe we can make her a bed in front of the coals for the night."

Lily had an old blanket that would serve, but she didn't want to leave to go fetch it. And it wasn't the coals Oceana was studying. Lily moved closer, feeling blind without their water connection. She couldn't see anything special about the scratched and dented soup kettle, but maybe if you'd lived your whole life in a ruin, it looked like treasure. "That's a pot. The water will stay warm overnight, and in the morning, Inga will add things and make a soup."

Oceana ignored her.

"Keep talking, missy, even if it looks like she isn't giving you the time of day. It will help remind her that people aren't rocks."

Some of them had rocks for brains, but she got his point. She opened her mouth to say something else, but her dragon was on the move again.

Straight toward the coals.

Lily dove and missed, landing face-first on the dirt floor as Oceana skittered straight up the stone hearth and in one swift, very wet move, leaped straight into the soup kettle. Lily jumped to her feet, reaching for the wildly swaying kettle and trying to keep her skirt out of the coals. She got one hand on the kettle and swiped her face with the other, clearing off the dirt and water that were rapidly turning to mud. "Oceana, you come out of there right this minute."

Her dragon rested her chin on the kettle's edge and chittered happily.

Lily glared and thrust her hand in the water. It was beautiful and warm. Not quite as warm as her hot pool, but close. And Oceana was practically exploding with contentment and pleasure.

Lily sighed. "You can't stay in there. You know that, right? Inga will kill us both."

Oceana just chittered again and laid her head on Lily's hand.

Behind them, Irin chuckled.

Lily sighed again and pulled up a stool, watching her dragon swim in happy circles in the soup pot. Life with a dragon definitely wasn't boring.

INTERLUDE

Lovissa shook her head as the dream faded, and tried not to puff any more smoke out her nose. Her cave stank of it, and no wonder.

The fate of dragonkind rested on a dragon who swam in a soup pot. Lovissa wanted to flick her tail over her eyes and hide, just like she'd done as a hatchling. It was mortifying. A dragon scared to fly had been bad enough, but if she were to tell her warriors of the Dragon Star's newest choice, the embarrassment would send them into battle with their tails between their legs.

Dragons were proud creatures—and at the very heart of their pride were the breaths of fire. Thus were dragons born and thus were their ashes given back to the Veld. One of their kind who scorned fire was beyond imagining.

Swimming. In a soup pot.

Lovissa let the thick, black humiliation settle on her shoulders. She could not tell her dragons of this new hope. Not until she knew more of the blue-green chosen one.

The dream had not all been dire. The small dragon had

bravery enough. The elf would not understand what it had cost to leave home, to leave all that was known.

As her dragons would need to do one day. Lovissa rumbled, and considered. Perhaps all hope was not lost after all. There were lessons to be learned from such courage. And perhaps a dragon who had never known fire, who had only known water, could be forgiven for embracing what lived all around her.

The elf was not weak like the last one, either. She spoke firmly, and her head had very little room for nonsense. Such a one could be a warrior, if she chose, much like the older man who had stood in the shadows. He was an elf Lovissa could almost respect.

If one could look past the smoke of humiliation, there were embers of hope. Lovissa let her eyelids slide back down, feeling better. To look in this way was a queen's job.

The small dragon would find fire. She was in a place of kin now, and she would learn. On that day, Lovissa would speak of the Dragon Star's second choice. Of the small one of courage and royal bearing, and perhaps some day of the elf who spoke with a gruffness that any warrior would appreciate.

Lily. Lovissa snorted. Such foolish names these elves had. Lilies were flowers, fragile things that wilted at the smallest whiff of fire. It didn't suit one of such fierceness.

Lovissa could feel slumber coming for her again, more peaceful this time. She tucked her tail a little more comfortably under her head.

Soup pots.

PART II
WATER & FIRE

CHAPTER 8

Lily perched on the small stool next to the rain barrel, leaned her head against the rondo at her back, and scowled at the first colors of the dawn lighting up the sky. This was a ridiculous hour to be up, but Kellen had shaken her awake while it was still the black of night. Something about needing to get the soup going and the bread rising before Inga arrived.

Which had somehow managed to get through the fog in Lily's head long enough for her to remember why she'd fallen asleep on a stool, wrapped in an old blanket, with her hand in a kettle.

She looked over at her dragon, sitting on top of the half-open rain barrel and watching the coming dawn with alert interest. "How did you manage to sleep so well, hmm?"

Mild amusement drifted through the water that joined them. Oceana preened, turning herself to catch the first rays of light on the large scales on her back.

"You're as vain as Alonia." Lily shook her head, which felt oddly light after days of wearing the copper headdress of her clan, and lifted up the plate on her lap. "Want some more of this meat pie before I finish it?" Kellen had spirited those out of some hidden location when she'd woken them up, since Oceana had eaten every single bite from the platters sometime in the night.

Oceana turned her face toward the sun and emitted a loud burp.

Lily snorted and took a large bite out of the meat pie. It might be the last one she saw for a while. Inga was bound to be grumpy about a dragon spending the night in her kitchen, even if that's all she found out. Lily had no idea what Kellen had done with the water in the kettle. Maybe today's soup would be dragon-flavored.

Lily rotated her head slowly, listening to the bones of her neck crack. First up on today's list was finding a bucket big enough for Oceana to sleep in—one that would fit beside a nice, comfortable bed for Lily.

"Morning." Sapphire's cheery voice emerged from the shadows, shortly followed by Sapphire herself holding up two mugs of something steaming. "Want some cider? Kellen said it will be a bit yet for bread, but she's got cheese and apples if you're hungry."

Lily offered the remnants of her meat pie to the peach-pink nose that was hiding behind Sapphire. "We'll wait for the bread, thanks." A rough tongue licked off her fingers, but Lotus wasn't the dragon Lily was watching. Oceana had snapped to attention, her eyes wide and suspicious and pointed straight at a peach-pink tail.

Sapphire rolled her eyes and half-turned. "You might as well stop hiding behind me, silly dragon."

That had been a lot easier when Lotus was small.

"She wanted to come visit." Sapphire was also keeping a watchful eye on Oceana's body language. "If we're all marked by the Dragon Star, I was thinking that maybe our dragons are meant to be friends."

That was a reasonable idea—and a terrifying one. Or it would be if Lily wasn't so sure the Dragon Star had been mistaken. After she managed a better night's sleep or two, she would figure out how to fix the error before anyone did anything foolish. Making friends, however, seemed like a good idea.

She sent calm through the water to Oceana. "Lotus causes the most trouble of any dragon who lives in the village, and she's the best flier here except for Fendellen." That was a point of major pride for both Sapphire and Lotus. "Sapphire is kin with Lotus, just like you are with me, and she likes water better than most elves."

Sapphire laughed. "I like your hot pool just fine. Swimming in the river in midwinter is for elves who've let their brains turn to berry mush."

It was a ritual of Lily's clan, and one the village never tired of teasing her about, but today wasn't a day to worry about that. Lily used her free hand to rub the scales of Oceana's tail as Lotus sidled closer. Making a friend in the village would be a good thing, especially if that friend was used to causing all the trouble and taking most of the blame. Sleeping in the soup kettle was tiny compared to some of the havoc Lotus had caused.

Oceana sent a picture that had Lily's eyebrows skittering up. She stared at her dragon. "Seriously?"

The picture never wavered.

Lily groaned. She eyed the peach-pink dragon. Lotus was generally willing to try anything once, the more harebrained the better. "Oceana would like you to put your tail in her rain barrel so that she can talk to you."

Sapphire's eyebrows went up. "Why can't she just talk to her mind?"

Lily shrugged. Her dragon didn't seem to work the way all the others did. "Maybe she can't, or maybe she doesn't want to." Oceana was emanating a curious feeling, and Lily suddenly want very much for this to work. "I think we need to try. She doesn't know how to make friends. She's probably never had one."

Sapphire's eyes looked worried. "Dragons don't like water. Maybe yours does, but that's going to be a hard way to make friends."

No one understood that better than a water-loving elf in a dragon kin village. Lily scowled. "I know that."

Lotus sidled a little closer to the rain barrel and then away again, like a small child who needed to use the outhouse but couldn't work out how to get inside. Sapphire put a hand on her shoulder, offering wordless encouragement.

Lotus lifted up her tail and moved it gingerly toward the water, and then yanked it away, blowing smoke and billowing dust. She quieted, looking embarrassed.

Lily kept a firm hand on Oceana. There would be no flying antics this morning, not before half the village was even awake.

Lotus tried again, and this time she almost got the very tip of her tail into the water. Then she whipped it away, making a scared chittering noise. Sapphire jumped to soothe her, kind words about bravery and trying hard and making new friends.

Lily stopped listening. Oceana had that distant feeling again, the one that said something deep inside her was trying to leave. Her dragon regarded Lotus for a long moment and then turned her back, curled up, and laid her head on her tail.

The tail that was no longer in the water, willing to make friends.

Something inside Lily shivered. This was not good. Not good at all.

"It's all right, younglings." Karis added her voice to Sapphire's soothing words. "That was a very good effort, Lotus, and there's no shame in trying your best and failing." A deep rumble sounded behind her.

Lily's eyes shot up. Afran almost never came into the village. He was huge, and even walking as gracefully as he could manage, his bulk put things at risk. His big head reached over one of the smaller rondos to peer at the rain barrel. ::You're a most beautiful color, dragon of the water. Greetings, and an honored welcome.::

Lily blinked, not at all sure how she was hearing his voice.

::I permit you to listen.:: Afran's gaze was focused on Oceana, who still faced away, but whose eyebrow ridges had perked up at the compliment. ::I have come to meet the newest Chosen.::

Lily winced at the title, but ignored it. They could talk

about the Dragon Star's mistakes later. "Will you stick your tail in her rain barrel?" That might help pull her dragon back from the empty place—and if anyone could do something most dragons hated, it would be Afran.

Even a light snort from the big dragon was enough to cover them all in dust.

Karis looked up at him, surprised. "That bad, huh?"

His scales writhed as the dragon shuddered. ::It is much as you would feel if I asked you to stick your hand in my fire.::

That brought images of cooking meat to mind that nearly made Lily sick. "It's just water. It won't hurt you."

"It's instincts," Irin said, walking over from the nursery. "Water puts out fire, and dragons have always regarded it as an enemy."

Afran puffed his agreement.

Irin reached a hand up to the big dragon's nose. "You can work your way up to it. You don't need to prove your bravery any more than Kis does."

::Kis is braver than I will ever be. This is not about courage. It is about honoring the request of the Chosen.::

They needed to stop calling Oceana that, and fast. Lily opened her mouth to say so, and then she realized a huge, hulking shadow was sneaking toward the rain barrel.

Afran's tail. And the dragon attached to it, the most valiant one she knew, was literally shaking in his boots.

It was crazy—but it was also working. Oceana's head lifted off her tail and pointed in Afran's direction. Her eyes were still lidded, but she felt more present. Less empty.

Lily held her breath. Surely Afran could do this.

The shadow came closer still, and it was clear it would

be a tight fit. Even the tip of his tail was nearly as big as the rain barrel itself.

Oceana scooted to her feet and plopped her tail in the water. Quivering. Eager.

Karis made a low moaning sound, her hands pasted to Afran's forehead. Trying to help him somehow.

A breath later, tail met water—and a rain barrel was in the air, water flying everywhere. Afran's tail smacked into a rondo and then into the puddle of water that had poured out of the barrel, sending mud flying after the water.

Lily spluttered as cold, slimy mud ran down her face. She tried to wipe it off with the sleeve of her tunic, with only marginal success. She peered through the mud. She couldn't see Oceana, but she could hear chittering from a nearby rooftop.

Very cranky chittering.

Afran's head hung almost to the ground, looking thoroughly chagrined.

"Well," said Karis, rubbing an arm across her own muddy face and speaking with a brightness that sounded forced. "That was a good effort. How about some breakfast?"

Alonia, who had apparently picked exactly the wrong time to come visit, scowled and looked down at the muddy, soaking-wet loaves in her hands. "That might need to wait a while."

Breakfast wasn't the only thing that was going to take a while. Lily looked up at the rondo roof where a blue-green dragon was already turning her back on the world, and tried not to worry.

CHAPTER 9

*L*ily tossed herself down on the only bench in the entire village that was in shade and took a huge bite of the sandwich she'd filched from the kitchen. Oceana was finally asleep, tucked in a shadowy corner of Lily and Alonia's rondo with a small pitcher of water for her tail and several mops nearby in case another mess happened.

Although to be fair, it hadn't been Oceana spilling most of the water today.

Alonia strolled over, her eyes brightening when she saw the other half of Lily's sandwich.

Lily tried not to grumble as she held it out. Alonia and Kellen had been working hard, trying to convince more dragons to stick their tails in a rain barrel.

Alonia blew curls off her face and shook her head as she sat down. "We can't find any others who are willing to try."

That wasn't a surprise—the last three candidates had all been teenager dragons like Lotus. Ones, as Afran put it, who didn't have all the brains in their heads yet. Brandel, the youngest of the three, had come the closest, but he'd also scorched the side of the nursery when he panicked. "Irin probably won't let us keep trying anyhow." He wasn't a fan of things in the village going up in flames.

"We could try the river," Alonia suggested softly. "Maybe they wouldn't feel quite so trapped that way."

It was a good idea—rivers were hard to set on fire. But it didn't do a lot to settle the churning in Lily's belly. She set down her sandwich, appetite suddenly gone. "We can't go down to the river every time Oceana wants to talk to another dragon." Or at least, when they wanted to talk to her. So far, besides Fendellen and Lily and elves bearing food, Oceana seemed to have very little interest in anyone else, scaled or not.

Alonia chewed, the sandwich filling her cheek. "Kellen's making berry pastries."

One of the few reliable ways to get Oceana's attention was with food. Which was a bit of a problem, because Lily couldn't cook to save her life. "Maybe I should go help."

Alonia shot her a skeptical look. "The last time you did that, we all had to eat burnt pastries."

That wasn't her fault. "Lotus trapped Inga in her rondo and I had to go help her escape."

"Really? Do you see other cooks out rescuing people?"

Not while they were waiting to take pastries out of the oven. Everyone had been very clear on the severity of that particular dereliction of duty. "Kellen's in charge. I could just help." Maybe it would help build the kin bond that still felt so very fragile. Irin said actions mattered.

Alonia's pat on her knee was kind. "You can help by

eating and getting your strength back for when your dragon wakes up."

That might be a long time. Oceana was an expert napper. "I'll go see if Karis needs any more help." Putting things right after Afran's mishap of the morning was probably done, but the big dragon was terribly embarrassed, and that might mean he needed his kin. Which meant Karis's usual chores would need to be done by somebody else.

"She's on her way to have a bath." Alonia's green eyes filled with merriment. "She said Afran's sulking, and she's not speaking to him again until he remembers he's a dragon and not a god."

The big dragon had very high standards for everyone's behavior, but none higher than the ones he held for himself. "Sapphire's pretty happy that Lotus doesn't hold the record for most impressive destruction of the village anymore."

Alonia laughed. "If Lotus finds out there's a competition for that, she might try to win it."

They looked at each other and winced, mostly in sympathy for their friend, who was forever cleaning up after her peach-pink menace—and then froze as a scream rang out.

Lily jumped to her feet as the door of the bathhouse rondo flew open and Karis bolted out, entirely naked, looking back over her shoulder and yelling like the demon hordes were after her.

Until she ran straight into Alonia, who had a sixth sense for the wrong places to stand this morning.

Somehow the two of them managed to stay upright—

and Karis stopped making the shrieking sounds that had brought everyone in the village running.

Kellen rushed up, holding out one of the big bathhouse towels.

Karis grabbed it, her cheeks turning pink and her eyes carefully avoiding anyone else's. She looked at the trail of water behind her instead as she wrapped the towel around her middle. When she spoke, her voice held its usual dry humor. "Well. It appears both my dragon and I have made quite a mess this morning."

Alonia giggled. "Afran's was way bigger."

Karis winked. "Perhaps we won't tell him that."

It was so weird to think of the large dragon as anything other than steady and wise. Lily edged closer, not at all sure how to help, but very familiar with being the butt of the villagers' stares. Friendly or not, it wasn't a good feeling.

Karis raised an eyebrow in Lily's direction. "Now that I'm not holding a cup of tea and trying to talk some sense into Afran as I climb into my bath, I suspect that the creature I mistook for a snake in my washtub is perhaps more simply explained."

No sane snake would ever come into a village full of dragons. Lily opened her mouth to say so and then realized what the rest of Karis's statement meant. "Oh, no."

Karis nodded wryly. "I do believe so."

That wasn't good. "She was asleep in our rondo—I only came out to eat."

"That does tend to be when our dragons decide to do something rash." Karis nodded calmly at the gathered villagers and put her hand on Kellen's shoulder. "That was fast thinking. Thank you."

Kellen flushed all the way to the roots of her hair. "I was already bringing towels to restock the bathhouse. I just happened to be nearby when you... um..."

Karis laughed. "Made an utter fool of myself?" She took the rest of the stack of towels from Kellen's arms. "How about I finish that job for you, shall I?" She glanced over her shoulder at Lily. "The two of us will go explain to Oceana that she will scare someone to death if she keeps hiding in every tub of warm water in the village."

Lily winced. Karis might forgive them. Inga most certainly wouldn't.

She followed her towel-clad teacher into the steamy bathhouse, blinking in the sudden dimness. A happy chitter sounded from deeper inside. Lily groaned. "You're going to be just as much trouble as Lotus."

"She just might be." Karis sounded amused. "The Dragon Star must have an unholy sense of humor."

That wasn't even a little bit funny. "I think it made a mistake."

"Oh, really?"

Lily knew skepticism when she heard it, even in the dark. "She hates fire and she doesn't even really like other dragons. And she's too small for us to fly to wherever the other dragons are." Periodic scouting parties flew out over the sea and limped back, and none had ever caught a glimpse of land. Oceana was a fast flyer, but she tired quickly. "I don't see how we could possibly be useful."

Karis grunted noncommittally.

Lily didn't really want to know what that meant, and right now she had more important things to attend to. Like the blue-green swamp creature currently paddling happily in the steaming tub that had been meant for Karis's bath.

Karis shook her head, watching Oceana's antics. "It's so very strange watching a dragon enjoy water that much."

Lily's belly wobbled. "Irin said Kis knew a story of other water dragons just like her."

"So he told me," Karis said gently. "Perhaps there were others of her kind once, or maybe they still exist in faraway lands."

There was no way she was traipsing around the known world seeking the remnants of a single tale remembered by a dragon who had been literally everywhere there was to go. Three days on the road with Oceana had been plenty. "She belongs here." For the first time, Lily was glad of the mark on her forehead that no one but Fendellen could see. "We're marked, so she must belong here."

"I have no doubt of that. Neither does Afran." Karis leaned against the high shelf that held bath towels and spare tunics. "But it won't be easy to help her fit in here."

Something in Karis's voice sounded as unsettled as whatever wobbled in Lily's belly. "We'll just have to work hard at it." Which sounded hollow, even to her ears. She'd been here for more than half her life, and fire still made her skin itch. Water and fire were things of instinct, and that didn't seem like something that would change very easily.

Oceana splashed with her tail, sending a rain shower of water out of the bath and over the rondo's occupants. Lily sighed. It was going to take work just to keep the village from turning into one big mudslide. "I'm sorry she got in your bathtub. I thought she was asleep."

Karis chuckled. "I'm used to dragon hijinks—I just didn't expect to find them in the bathhouse." Her forehead wrinkled in thought. "I think the bigger issue might be that Oceana won't feel settled in a rondo."

Lily made a face. "Not unless we put a pond in ours, and Alonia won't like that idea very much."

Karis snorted, amused. "It might be a bit of a hazard in the middle of the night."

It couldn't possibly be more of a problem than a dragon who snuck into bathtubs and soup pots. If Inga got startled and ran through the village naked, the consequences would be dire. "I don't know how to help her feel more comfortable." The village wasn't set up for anyone who loved water—nobody knew that better than Lily. Her friends had put out buckets of water everywhere they could think of, but that didn't really hide that the village was entirely set up to be welcoming to dragons of the fire-loving kind.

Karis raised an eyebrow. "Have you taken her down to your warm pool? I could ask Afran to heat it for you."

Lily ducked as Oceana splashed with her tail again. "I thought about it, but I might never get her out." Their bond felt really fragile to deal with that kind of temptation. Getting her dragon out of the soup pot had been hard enough.

"Maybe you don't need to." Karis hummed, thinking. "We could set up one of the travel tents down there. They aren't nearly as warm as a rondo, but the nights are warm yet."

It sounded like a good idea—but something inside Lily wasn't happy. It felt too much like being evicted from the village. "How can she get used to being here if we take her away?"

"It's not far." Karis got the vacant look that said she was talking with her dragon. "We can all come down to visit. Afran says there's a nice grassy spot close by. He can come and breathe fire while Oceana is in the pool. Maybe that way she'll feel less nervous."

Lily crossed her arms, not sure why she wasn't in love with this idea. Possibly she was just cranky. It had been a very long night of sleeping on a stool and an even longer morning of watching her dragon's abject failure to make friends. If Oceana liked the warm pool, at least they could both get a decent night's sleep. She nodded. "Could Afran warm it up, please? He's better than anyone." Which was true, and it might also help soothe his embarrassment.

"Already done." Karis smiled. "Go show your dragon her new bathtub."

CHAPTER 10

*L*ily threw an arm over her face, protesting the sun in her eyes. It couldn't possibly be morning yet, and morning was never this bright. Her bed was very specifically placed to avoid just this eye-aching occurrence.

Then she remembered that her bed had been moved, carried down to the waterside tent by several helpful villagers. Lily was pretty sure they'd just wanted the latest troublesome dragon cleared out of town. She ratcheted one eye open, looking for the distinctive blue-green of the troublemaker she'd bonded with. Instead, she discovered she was staring up at the roof of the tent, and her left arm felt very strange.

She found enough wits to roll toward the limb that was hanging off the edge of the bed, lifting her numb fingers up and peering at them. They were wet. There shouldn't be water in her tent. She blinked, trying to get the gears in her head to do something other than clank together and make a lot of noise. Then she spied the small, rock-lined channel of water that ran right in the open side of the tent and stopped at the edge of her bed.

That had been Kellen's idea.

Lily vaguely remembered lying down for a nap before dinner, fingers in the channel, comforted by the sleepy feel of her dragon settling in for a nap of her own. She cast a glance at the sky. They were well into the middle of the morning, which meant she'd slept through dinner, a full night, and a good chunk of the next day besides.

She peered at her fingers, which were as soggy as pond-frog toes, and stuck them back in the water. Still surprisingly warm. And happily, containing a dragon. One who was most certainly not asleep, however.

At least she wasn't off haunting somebody's bathtub. Lily stretched, groaned, rubbed her eyes, and managed to swing her feet off the bed. The ground felt cool under her bare toes. She rubbed her eyes one more time and stood, walking to the edge of the tent.

A low chirring sound, almost like a purr, greeted her. Oceana, lounging on a flat rock at the edge of the pool, tail in the water, soaking in the morning sun.

Lily greeted curious black eyes and felt more solid than she had in days. Those were eyes that were happy to see her, no matter how precarious their bond felt. She sat down beside the flat rock and reached one hand for a scaled chin, the other into the water. "Good morning, sleepyhead."

Two puffy snorts that felt like laughter.

It lifted something in Lily's chest. "You've been up since the crack of dawn, have you?" She cast a glance at a low wood block just inside the tent and the sparkling clean plate sitting on it. "I suppose that means you ate my dinner."

Three snorts this time—and a very clear vision of what the plate had looked like before all the food had disappeared.

Lily raised a stern eyebrow, but it was hard not to be amused. "You were supposed to share that."

Another picture, this one of Lily flat on her back in the bed, one arm dangling over the edge, snoring as loudly as a bear.

Lily groaned and hoped that one was an exaggeration. "Let's get clean, and then we can wander up to the village for some breakfast." However nice sleeping by a pool of warm water might be, it lacked most of the other basic necessities of life, including something for her rumbling belly.

Oceana stretched out and lowered her head onto the rock.

Lily stroked her dragon's eye crests with a firm finger, just how Lotus liked it. "You'd rather stay here, would you?" Not a surprise, but a worry. The pool was beautiful, but in some ways, it felt a bit like moving to a fancier ruin. Out of the way. Excluded. Which was the last thing her dragon needed.

Lily sighed and set her chin on her knees. It wasn't really what a cranky water elf needed either. She'd worked hard to become a welcome and necessary part of the village. This felt like a big step backwards in her own life too.

She picked her chin back up. This was only temporary,

until they could get Oceana more used to fire-breathing dragons. And at least it came with good swimming. She slid her fingers back into the water. "I'll go get us some breakfast. You stay right here."

"That won't be necessary."

The gruff voice from behind had her turning in surprise. Irin walked down the low rise, bearing a tray in one hand and a pitcher in the other. He nodded at her, and at the small dragon on the rocks. "Kellen thought the two of you might be hungry."

Oceana watched him carefully, but she didn't move.

Progress. Lily ran over to take the pitcher, inhaling the smell of warm spiced cider. It would go perfectly with the food piled high on the tray. Bread, cheese, hardboiled eggs, a bowl of spiced stew meat, and at least half a dozen fruit pastries. Plenty to tempt a hungry dragon and her elf.

Irin set the tray down on a low rock and casually sat down between Oceana and the food.

Lily grinned—apparently he was smarter than she was when it came to leaving food unsupervised. She slid a thick slice of cheese between two pieces of bread, tucked her makeshift sandwich in one hand, and held out a piece of spiced stew meat to Oceana with the other.

Her dragon sniffed and wrinkled her nose, eyeing the bread and cheese instead.

Irin chuckled. "Kellen figured she wouldn't like that. Hot and spicy. Too much like fire."

Kellen was seriously smart. Lily broke off a piece of fruit pastry instead. They already knew Oceana liked those.

"You can save the stew for Kis." Irin leaned back against a rock. "It's one of his favorites."

Lily looked up from her food, wide-eyed. "Kis is coming here?" The old dragon rarely left the nursery. His war wounds pained him too much, and Lily was pretty sure the sight of the open sky he couldn't fly in anymore did too.

Irin nodded slowly. "He is. Something about a job that needed a warrior to get it done right."

Irin's face was solemn, but his eyes looked pleased. Lily swallowed her mouthful of bread and cheese and looked at her dragon. Kis might not be able to fly, but he was as full of fire as any dragon she knew. "What's he going to do?" Helping Oceana fit into the village didn't seem like a job for a dragon who puffed smoke every time he got irritated —which was most of the time.

"He's coming to talk to her." Irin reached for a slice of bread and cheese.

Lily gulped. Oceana's head shot up, looking over the warm pool to the large clearing on the other side. The one that had been specifically made big enough for the dragons who came to heat the pool. They could hear the sounds of branches and grasses trampled under a heavy, moving body.

Lily scrambled to her feet just in time to see Kis reach the edge of the clearing. He walked with a tilt, favoring his most tattered wing and a leg that had once held so many arrows it had resembled a pincushion.

He didn't resemble one now. He lumbered into the clearing, the bright morning sun at his back turning his yellow scales a burnished gold color.

Lily smiled at his golden eyes. "You look really beautiful today."

Irin snorted. "Keep insulting him and he'll turn right back around and leave."

Lily didn't take her words back. All dragons liked to be told they were pretty, even the toughest ones. Alonia proved that every single day. Kis looked almost proud, arching his neck to catch the best light.

Irin snorted again. "Fine, you old boot. You don't look terrible, for once."

Lily snuck a glance at Oceana, who curled up at attention on her rock, but didn't show any immediate signs of taking to sky, water, or the forest beyond. Which was good, because Fendellen wasn't around to chase her anymore. Belatedly, Lily remembered her manners and dropped into a crouch, putting her fingers in the water. "Oceana, this is Kis, revered dragon warrior and kin to Irin." Then she eyed the big dragon and let herself feel proud too. "Kis, this is Oceana. She is my dragon."

The words hung in the air, feeling deep and important. Oceana wasn't at all distant. She paid absolute attention, and her eyes hadn't left the big dragon shining in the morning light. Slowly, she sat up and flared her neck crest, turning it to catch the rays of the sun just as Kis had done.

Irin snorted, but very quietly. "Really, old man? *That's* what you're going to teach her first?"

Kis blew an impressive amount of smoke out his nose.

Oceana hissed, and Lily dove to grab her before she went anywhere. She wrapped her arms around her quivering dragon and held on tight. "It's just smoke." She glared at Kis. "He won't make fire unless he warns us first."

Irin leaned back against his rock, clearly leaving this lesson, whatever it was, up to Kis.

The old dragon tilted his head and snorted smoke again.

Oceana hissed, but it wasn't quite as determined this time.

Irin suddenly sat up straighter, lifted an eyebrow at the gold dragon. "Don't push it, old man. This isn't weapons training on the battlefront."

Those were scary words from a man who regularly scared the demons out of all of them. Lily eyed Kis. There was only one reason Irin would be that alarmed. "He's going to breathe fire, isn't he?"

"Yes." Irin's voice had the kind of calm it always had right before a storm. "He wants to heat up the water again. Says it's gone cold."

It was still nicely lukewarm, but Lily knew exactly how futile it was to get a cranky dragon to change his mind. She clamped down on the squirming dragon in her arms and nodded at Kis. They might as well get it over with. "Maybe he can toast me a cheese sandwich while he's at it." Lotus did that sometimes, and the melted cheese on the crunchy bread was one of her favorite treats.

Maybe Oceana would like it too.

Irin started to shake his head and stopped, casting her a surprised glance. "That's not bad thinking, missy."

Lily gritted her teeth. She wasn't an entirely brainless elf. Food was the way to her dragon's heart—or it had been thus far, at least. She loosened her grip on Oceana while Irin quickly soaked a stick and impaled some bread and cheese on the end.

Lily blinked at his efficient movements. Clearly they weren't the first ones to have discovered dragon-toasted sandwiches.

Ready, he held it up and nodded at his dragon. Lily took a good, firm hold of hers, catching her breath as the clicks that came before fire sounded in the clearing. Then the billowing heat as a very focused stream of fire shot into the pond, cutting off just as the water started to steam.

Irin deftly caught the falling sandwich on a plate and waved a charred stick at Kis. "Nicely done."

Lily dared a look down at her arms. Oceana was a frozen dragon statue. One staring at Kis, with her tail in the water—the water that had just gone from lukewarm to steaming in a single breath.

Slowly, Lily let go just enough to free her fingers and put them in the water—and nearly drowned in what she felt. Blazing terror, and just underneath it, a wild kind of awe. She pushed calm at Oceana. Steadiness. The knowledge that this was something that happened with regularity and was nothing to fear.

Very slowly, the shaking subsided, and gratefully, Lily let her hold on Oceana ease. It was a bit like cuddling a porcupine. Every spike on her dragon's body stuck straight up, and most of them had found Lily's soft parts to poke. Gingerly, she let go of Oceana entirely, but kept her fingers in the water.

Kis's eyes seemed to regard her fingers, and then the old dragon began to move. One lumbering step and then another. Oceana quivered, but she wasn't nearly so scared anymore. Lily let her be. She couldn't hold her dragon down all the time.

Kis closed the distance to the edge of the pond and began to lie down, looking for all the world like he was going to take a nap.

Lily stared. No dragon other than Lotus had ever gotten that close to the pool. Most of them couldn't even make it into the clearing—they mostly chose to heat the water from the sky. "He looks totally calm."

"He's not," Irin said very quietly. "But unlike the others who have tried this, he knows what it is to take to the skies even when you're deathly afraid. He knows the water won't hurt him. It's only fear he has to conquer."

Lily watched the dragon she mostly thought of as a bedtime storyteller lower himself ungracefully to the ground, one awkward, painful bend at a time.

Oceana's chin moved forward a little. Toward Kis.

The old dragon ignored her, going through the slow, aching motions needed to curl up at the edge of the pool, his unblinking golden eyes never looking away from the water. Staring down an adversary. Showing no fear.

Irin growled softly, and it was a sound full of pride.

Kis paused a long moment, and then his tail began to move. Not with pain this time. There were no jerking movements—just the smooth remnants of skill that had once been the finest flyer in the sky. Lily held her breath as yellow-gold scales descended toward the mists and the water.

Oceana's chin moved forward a little more.

When the tip of Kis's tail slid into the water, a great shudder shook his whole body.

Irin inhaled sharply. "You've got this, old man."

The shudder lessened, a great dragon throwing off the

fetters of fear as he let a length of his tail as long as Lily was tall slide into the water. The shaking gone, he looked across the pool, golden eyes meeting Irin's brown ones first, and then Lily's, and finally the shiny black ones of a small dragon held entirely still by nothing but awe.

Kis rumbled softly, the same sound he made when he lulled Lotus to sleep.

Oceana chittered with startled excitement.

Kis rumbled again, and this time Irin chuckled. "He says the water feels good."

Oceana whirred and splashed her tail on the surface of the water. The droplets fell nowhere near Kis, but he glared sternly and snorted smoke out his nose anyhow.

Lily hid a giggle as her dragon bowed her head exactly like a small child who had just been scolded. Splashing Kis was a *very* bad idea. Then Oceana lifted her head and tried to blow smoke out her own nose, spraying her flat rock with snot instead.

Kis made a noise that sounded for all the world like laughter.

Oceana stood, preening in the sun for a moment, and then slid into the water without splashing at all. She paddled as far as the middle of the pool and swam in small circles, her eyes never leaving the golden dragon on the far side.

Irin leaned back, crossing his legs and holding out one half of the toasted sandwich.

Lily took it and let the melted cheese feed the glow she felt inside.

CHAPTER 11

Lily stretched in her bed and squinted her eyes against the morning sun. She could get used to this. Waking up to this kind of brightness meant you'd slept right through the village crashing about getting ready to greet the day.

She blew out a breath and sat up, shaking off her wet fingers. Today didn't feel as lonely and uncertain as yesterday. Kis's visit had convinced her that maybe this was possible, that Oceana could figure out how to live around dragons that snorted smoke as often as most people cleared their throats. They'd taken the first step, and it was Irin who always said that was the hardest one.

Lily grimaced. That man thought way too many steps in life needed to be hard. But she wouldn't hold it against him. Not today while the sun shone and his dragon had become Oceana's first friend.

A stray giggle squirted out into the morning. Kis was normally the farthest thing from a warm and welcoming dragon in the existence of dragons. But when he'd finally lumbered home yesterday, Irin had muttered something under his breath about the day having been a good one for two dragons, and Lily believed him.

Maybe they could eventually teach him to splash his tail in the pool.

She shook her head ruefully and stood up. They'd have to move the tent first.

She grinned at Oceana, still sound asleep on a rock, and made it as far as the closed basket that hadn't been there the night before, when she heard a very familiar noise headed their way. A part of the village clatter she'd actually missed. She could hear Kellen's voice, teasing, and Alonia's lilting, dismissive reply. Sapphire laughed and exchanged words with a deeper voice Lily couldn't quite make out.

She looked down at the basket and hoped it held enough breakfast to feed company too.

It was Karis's head she spied first, taller than the three she walked with. Lily felt oddly protective of her dragon. Karis was a very good teacher, but Oceana's first lesson with Afran had been a bit of a disaster.

Kellen grinned and held up a basket that matched the one by Lily's tent door. "Good morning, sleepyheads."

Her head did still feel pretty sleepy. "Hi. Thanks for coming to eat with us." Maybe exile by the warm pool wouldn't be so bad.

"We're not here as breakfast guests." Karis took a seat on a flat rock. "Lessons don't end just because you have a dragon. You've missed nearly a fortnight with the wedding trip and the rest of your excitement."

Alonia scowled. "We missed the wedding."

Karis chuckled. "I would find that the preferable outcome, but I understand your sadness at missing something you'd looked forward to."

Kellen handed Alonia a berry pastry still dripping with juices. "You're just mad you didn't get to wear your best dress."

Lily was glad someone was taking over the teasing in her absence. Alonia came from a clan of talkers, and she tended to feel abandoned if there weren't several verbal sword fights a day.

Karis calmly reached for a berry pastry of her own. "Word has traveled that Oceana let Kis warm her pool yesterday. Lotus is going to come by and do the same this morning." She held up a hand as Lily started to protest. "Just the warming. For now, we'll leave Kis with the fine distinction of being the only dragon brave enough to put his tail in the water."

Good. Lily had seen how Lotus reacted to a few stray drops of water, and it wasn't pretty, but she had always been willing to heat the water for them, generally from as far up in the sky as she could get and still have decent aim.

Karis studied Oceana, who had woken up and was watching the visitors alertly. "We'll have to see if she can talk to the dragons some other way."

Lily bit into her berry pastry harder than she needed to. "She talks through water."

"I know." Karis nodded. "And if that's the only way she can speak to another dragon, we'll figure out how to manage. But her world will get a lot more comfortable and full of company if she can learn to speak mind to mind like the other dragons do. Afran thinks she may just need lessons."

The words gritted on Lily's skin, no matter how reasonably they'd been spoken. "She can't speak to my mind without water, and we're bonded."

Karis looked a little grimmer at that thought. "True."

Kellen tilted her head. "There was a man in my clan who couldn't hear, and he used his hands to speak."

Karis gave her a pleased smile. "That's an option as well."

Lily shoved her whole fruit pastry in her mouth. She wanted to yell at them all. Oceana was easy to talk to—you just had to put a finger or a tail in the water. It wasn't her fault that all the other dragons were scared of something that couldn't hurt them.

When she finally swallowed, all three of her friends were looking at her anxiously.

Lily tried to breathe around all the pastry crumbs. She couldn't help Oceana if she lost her temper every time someone had an idea. "Kis managed to put his tail in the water. Maybe the other dragons can learn too."

"Maybe." Karis looked skeptical. "But in this case, we have one water dragon and hundreds of fire dragons. It would be much simpler to help Oceana learn new ways."

Spoken like someone who didn't know what it was like to feel all dry and itchy every time a dragon breathed fire. Lily swallowed. Kis had breathed fire at Oceana, but he'd done it to warm her water and toast her sandwich. And he'd put his tail in her pool and kept it there long enough for Lily to get hungry again.

This felt different, all the hard parts with nothing to

balance them. Oceana already knew how to be an outcast. They needed to help her want to belong.

"You look worried." Karis's voice was steady and kind.

Lily shrugged. "It seems like all we're talking about is my dragon's problems." The invisible mark on her forehead itched and made her want to scratch.

Sapphire sighed. "At least people aren't asking why the Dragon Star chose you."

Maybe they should be. "I think it was a mistake."

Sapphire grinned. "I thought that too."

Lily tried again. Lotus had been a menace, but it had been obvious that she was special right from the very first day. "You just had to get brave about flying. I have a dragon who is way too small for me to ride, and all she wants to do is sleep and eat meat pies and maybe go back to her swamp." She slapped a hand to her mouth. She hadn't meant to say that last part. She hadn't really meant to say any of it.

It was Kellen who moved first, sliding in to give her a hug. "She's just homesick. We all were when we got here, remember? It doesn't mean anything is wrong."

Alonia smiled, chin on her knees, and looked right at Oceana. "I think she's the most beautiful dragon here. Her scales are a color I've never seen before, and they look like the sky and the spring green leaves all at the same time."

Oceana preened a little on her rock.

Lily jerked, surprised her dragon had understood—and then saw Alonia's fingers trailing in the water.

One friend who got it. Most people thought Alonia only had half a brain, but they were wrong. Lily shot her a grateful glance and turned to face Karis. If her friends could stand up for her dragon, surely she could do the same.

"Stand down, youngling." Karis gave her a wry look. "I'm not the enemy, and I will help you and your dragon to the very best of my abilities. Starting with this. You worry that your dragon's weaknesses, and perhaps your own, mean the Star chose incorrectly."

Lily hadn't even said that last part to herself, but it was true. She was a strange elf with a bad temper who couldn't cook and didn't like fire—or most people. "I don't understand why we would have been chosen."

Karis shrugged. "I don't either."

Somehow, the honesty was reassuring.

"I do know this." Karis leaned back against a log Lily had dragged over the previous night and included all four of them in her gaze. "Sapphire and Lotus's biggest weakness became their strength."

Sapphire smiled shyly.

Lily snorted. Her friend didn't need to be shy. Those two flew circles around practically everyone else in the sky. Then she realized what Karis was really saying and frowned. "You think Oceana and I need to turn fire into our strength?" She could hear her voice getting higher, like someone was squeezing her around the middle.

"Possibly—or at least the facing of it." Karis's eyes were steady, but they didn't let Lily look away. "Afran believes that the five may be learning lessons they will one day need to teach."

Lily wrinkled her nose. This conversation was making less and less sense. "The old dragons aren't scared of fire."

Not unless all the ballads and stories were big, fat lies, anyhow.

"No," Karis said quietly. "But they are scared of elves."

The dragons who had picked up the old queen's star message all used stronger words than that. "They're at war. They hate the elves."

"Oh." Kellen let out a soft, surprised breath. "Then Karis is right. That will need to change. The five who will save them aren't just dragons. They're elves, too."

Karis nodded slowly. "Imagine that Oceana was in trouble and her rescuer tried to use fire to save her."

Slow horror dawned in Lily's ribs. "She wouldn't let them help."

Karis met her eyes. "Sapphire and Lotus needed to overcome their biggest fear. I don't think that was an accident. It may be something all of the five will need to do so you can help the old dragons face that which they fear most."

Lily groaned and tucked her head down between her knees. "Couldn't I just learn to cook? That would be so much easier."

Kellen started giggling, and pretty soon Alonia and Sapphire joined her. Lily raised her head and scowled at them all.

She wasn't *that* terrible in the kitchen. And fire wasn't *that* scary. She would help Oceana. Together, they would learn.

CHAPTER 12

Lily winced as Oceana shot up the inside of her tunic. Again. She grabbed for whatever dragon parts she could find. Elf skin wasn't nearly as tough as dragon scales, something Oceana seemed to forget entirely in the presence of fire.

Even fire so far away they could barely see it.

She squinted at the two young dragons in the sky off in the distance, blowing fire at each other and probably scaring the cows while they were at it, especially since a certain peach-pink dragon didn't aim her fire all that well when she was barrel rolling. Lily looked over at Sapphire.

"Can you ask Lotus to stop until I get this creature out from under my clothes?"

Sapphire laughed. "I can *ask*."

Lily rolled her eyes and peeled clenched blue claws out of her skin. Blowing fire within sight of the village was rarely a permissible activity, and Lotus had been taking full advantage of the new rules, much to the dismay of the more rule-bound dragons, villagers, and cows. Inga was convinced they'd get no more butter this summer, and Lily couldn't really blame the cows. Fire was nasty stuff.

She tried to keep that thought to herself. Her emotions didn't seem to impact Oceana all that much, but there was no point in reinforcing behaviors they were trying to change. She didn't want to spend any more time as an elf pincushion than absolutely necessary.

Kellen, in charge of food bribes, held out a bite of bread and cheese for Oceana. A pink tongue emerged from under Lily's tunic and licked it up.

Lily sighed. Unless their job was to teach the dragons of old how to eat, they were doomed to be abject failures as star-chosen ones. "Maybe we should take a break and try again in a while." She eyed the elf sitting in the shade supervising this training session. Karis tended to frown on unscheduled pauses.

Their teacher raised a stern eyebrow. "A short one."

Lily grimaced. Sometimes Karis looked awfully like her dragon.

Kellen tugged on Lily's elbow. "We'll go get some more snacks from the kitchen. That can be part of the lesson, because it will help Oceana get used to the village."

Lily frowned. Taking Oceana anywhere near the kitchen was a bad idea, but Kellen knew that. Which meant she was up to something. Fortunately, Karis didn't appear to be thinking hard enough to have figured that out. Lily adjusted the dragon-shaped lump under her tunic and followed in Kellen's footsteps.

They walked silently for a bit, looping around the village. Lily thought they might be headed back to the pool when Kellen abruptly turned and ducked through the trees that shaded the kitchen gardens in the late afternoon.

Oceana's head popped out the top of her tunic. Lily contemplated stopping by a rain barrel, but her dragon's eyes seemed interested, not scared, which was a large improvement over the morning thus far. So she looked over at Kellen instead. "Where exactly are you dragging us?"

Kellen looked a little abashed, maybe even nervous. "I have a different idea for the fire lessons."

Lily blinked. "Why didn't you say so?"

Her friend shrugged. "Because I'm not sure if it will work, and I didn't want to make anybody mad."

Nobody questioned Afran and Karis, not when it came to matters of teaching and learning. They were legendary for their wisdom, patience, and skill with hard heads.

Kellen reached for Lily's arm and tugged as they made it past the last of the flourishing soup greens. Lily's eyebrows flew up as she realized where they were headed —and why her dragon was suddenly looking so cheerful. "We're going to visit Kis?"

Kellen nodded.

Nobody visited Kis unannounced. "He's probably napping." Irin was off with a couple of the youngest students trying to keep the cows calm, and the old dragon needed a lot of sleep because of his war wounds.

"He's not," Kellen said calmly. "I took him some breakfast this morning and asked him to be ready for our visit."

Lily's respect for Kellen's daring jumped up several notches. "You *planned* this?"

Kellen might be little, but she knew plenty about

looking fierce. "I did. I took his favorite spicy stew so he'd be in a good mood."

The cranky old dragon wouldn't ordinarily be anyone's choice as a teacher, but he'd been wonderful with Oceana down at the pool. Lily tilted her head, considering. "You think he can teach her to tolerate fire?"

"I don't know." Kellen shrugged. "I think she likes him, and maybe she even trusts him a little. I set up one of the old kitchen pots in there, and he's going to heat it up so she can have a nice, warm bath."

Lily stared at her friend as they ducked into the nursery, and then at the pot standing in the middle of the rondo, suspended from one of the iron tripods they used in the big kitchen hearth. "What if Irin had found this before we got here?"

Kellen shrugged. "Then he would have yelled at me and put it back in the storage shed where I got it from, or maybe Kis would have been able to convince him that this is an idea worth trying."

Lily looked over at the massive yellow dragon, who looked sound asleep. "You talked about all of this with Kis?" The old dragon was one of the few capable of speaking to anyone in the village, but he rarely bothered.

"Yes." Kellen's smile was small, but proud. "He said I might make a fine teacher one day."

That was possibly the nicest thing she'd ever heard come out of the cranky old dragon's mouth. Lily smiled. She'd dodged Kis's fire more times than she could count, but maybe he was turning over a new leaf. And anything sounded better than having Oceana crawl up her skin over and over again.

Kellen firmly shut the nursery door, which would at least slow down Oceana's exit. Lily looked down at the black eyes that were very close to her nose and walked over to the kitchen pot, sticking her fingers in the cool water. "We're in a safe place now, and you need to come out of there. Crawling up under my clothes hurts, and you're not a baby dragon who needs to hide."

Oceana looked a little abashed and dropped her tail in the water. The picture she sent was one of the soothing dim inside her ruins. Safety.

Lily rolled her eyes. "You like the daylight just fine when it makes your sleeping rock warm. My tunic isn't a cave." She looked around the rondo. "It's plenty dim in here, so out from under my clothes." She tapped a blue-green nose for emphasis.

A darting pink tongue licked her finger, and then Oceana scooted out the bottom of her tunic.

Kellen giggled and held out a length of frayed rope.

Lily looked at it, puzzled. "What's that for?"

"A belt." Kellen grinned. "That way, she won't be able to crawl up your insides."

That was genius—and so obvious, Lily was a little disgruntled that nobody had thought of it a lot sooner. She took the rope and wound it around her waist twice, tying it off in a simple knot.

Oceana walked across the nursery floor like she owned the place and butted her head up against Kis's side, scratching her head spikes against his huge scales.

Lily winced and reached for her dragon. Waking Kis was never a good idea.

A rumble froze her in her tracks. "She's fine." A golden

eye slid open and surveyed the two of them. "I promise not to set her on fire unless she gets really annoying."

Oceana chittered at him, obviously glad to see her friend awake, and jumped up on the kitchen pot, sticking her tail inside.

Lily wasn't sure what to do. There was no way Kis's tail was going to fit in the pot, even if he wanted to put it there—and that was doubtful.

The old dragon gazed at them, his eye unblinking. "Perhaps if you put your fingers in the water, she could hear me through your kin bond."

Lily shook her head. There was no point having good ideas fail twice. "We already tried that with Afran."

Kis snorted. "He's more of an old man than I am some days. All right. Then I'll talk to you, and you can pass my words to your dragon."

Lily blinked. That was another one of those obvious ideas no one had thought of.

Kis's visible eye looked mildly amused. "Soldiers rarely all speak the same language. A leader's words on the battlefield are often relayed by others."

A lump formed in Lily's throat. That was exactly it. Oceana spoke a different language, and Kis was the first one to see it that way instead of as some kind of deformity. "Thank you."

Kis snorted smoke again. Oceana chittered, and this time it wasn't a happy sound. The old dragon looked straight at her. "No back talk from you, missy. I'm working on learning your language and customs, and you darn well need to get used to mine."

Eyes wide, Lily thrust her fingers into the water and

repeated his words under her breath.

Oceana startled and looked back and forth between them.

"I'm giving you his words." Lily stroked a ridge crest. "And he's right. He was brave enough to stick his tail in your water. Now you need to show him you can be just as brave."

Her dragon blinked slowly, studying the old dragon.

Kis lifted his head. "I may be a useless old fart who sleeps all day and hurts far too much, but I can aim fire better than any dragon still living, and most of the dead ones too."

Lily passed on the words, wondering why that wasn't a thing she had known.

Kellen stepped forward, looking nervous. "Are you sure you can do this in here, Kis? I can move the pot outside."

"And make me get up and walk all the way out there?" Kis harrumphed. "You made a good battle plan, youngling. Have a little faith in your soldiers."

Lilly passed on all the words quietly, noting just how interested Oceana's eyes had become.

Kis raised his head, stretching his jaw in a way that was truly terrifying. Oceana hissed at him. He hissed right back. "Manners, missy, or I'll scorch your scales."

Lily winced as she transmitted. Threatening a dragon scared of fire with being scorched seemed kind of harsh.

Kis never took his eyes off his student, but Lily could have sworn that his rumble sounded the tiniest bit amused.

Oceana sat up straight as a rod on the edge of the soup pot, eyes glued to the big dragon.

Kellen tugged Lily away from pot. Reluctantly, she

went. Elves weren't nearly as fireproof as dragons.

Kis gave no warning. No words, no clicks in his throat. Just a hot, tight stream of flame straight onto the bottom of the metal pot.

It was done before Lily could even squeak. She stared at the steaming pot and at her dragon sitting like a statue on the edge of it. She dashed forward, thrusting her fingers into the pot, and winced. It was almost hot enough to cook soup, but Oceana's tail hadn't moved. And the feeling in the water wasn't terror.

It was awe. And maybe even a touch of gratitude.

Oceana slid into the steaming pot, and the feeling running up Lily's fingers turned to bliss. She raised her eyebrows at her dragon. "You're going to turn into dragon soup."

A snort behind them warned that they had a visitor. Or rather, the man who considered the nursery his domain. Lily turned, carefully keeping her fingers in the water.

Irin scowled at all of them, but mostly at his dragon. "You blew fire. In my nursery."

One of Kis's eyebrow ridges slid up.

Irin snorted. "Fine, *our* nursery. But I'm the one who'd be doing all the work to rebuild it if you burned it down."

Rondos didn't burn very easily, and Kis had aimed his fire really well. Lily opened her mouth to say so when she felt an odd squeezing motion in her head. ::I'm not old enough to need puny elves to fight my battles for me, missy.::

Lily didn't say a word as an old dragon and old warrior went back to glaring at each other. She somehow wasn't surprised when it was Irin who blinked first.

CHAPTER 13

Lily stared at her dragon, who was sitting with her tail in the water, calmly facing down Karis and Afran and making a very clear pronouncement. One that wasn't going over well at all.

Oceana had apparently learned a different lesson in the nursery rondo than the intended one. She'd learned that sometimes rebellion worked, and that old dragons who put their feet down were very hard to move.

Lily sighed and shook her head at Karis. "She's not changing her mind."

Karis gave the small blue-green dragon a wry look. "No more fire lessons unless they involve Kis and a bath?"

Even those were just barely acceptable terms. Lily winced. This was not a case where it was fun to be the messenger.

Karis frowned and trailed her fingers in the water of the warm pool. Lotus had heated it this morning. Oceana had issued edicts there too. Afran wasn't allowed to blow fire at her pool.

Lily held her silence. Their teacher was thinking, and that was hopefully a good thing. Irin would be yelling by now, but Karis was calmer, even if she was every bit as tough.

Karis raised her eyebrows and looked sternly at Oceana. "For now, Kis will be in charge of your fire lessons. You will also have lessons with Afran in dragon lore and history." She glanced at Lily. "Your kin will stay with you and translate."

Lily reached for another slice of bread and tried not to groan. Dragon lore and history were interesting enough the first time through, but she could probably recite them in her sleep by now. "I could do some of that with her. We don't need Afran for all of it."

::It is not for elves to teach the history of dragonkind::

Afran sounded almost annoyed. It was Karis who had Lily's attention, though. Their teacher was staring at Oceana, bemused and trying not to laugh.

Lily hastily stuck her fingers back in the water—and then slapped her other hand, bread and all, over her mouth as she caught the tail end of her dragon's reply. The one with a crystal-clear picture of Afran talking and Oceana lying on a rock, sound asleep, complete with a rumbling snore. A single giggle snuck out around the bread. Lily shook her head at her cheeky dragon. Afran would *not* be amused.

"He isn't," Karis said dryly. "But apparently, Oceana's skill extends to talking to other dragon kin. Or perhaps beyond that." She motioned to Kellen, who had brought down breakfast and stood hiding in the shadows, trying to offer moral support while staying out of the way of annoyed dragons. "Here, see if she can speak to you."

Kellen's eyes lit up. She moved to the water's edge and dipped her fingers in. "Hello, pretty girl. What would you like for breakfast?"

Lily could feel that her dragon didn't understand, so she repeated the words. Karis nodded, as if her suspicions had just been confirmed.

Oceana tilted her head and sent back a very clear picture of berry pastries. Kellen grinned and jumped up. "I brought some of those."

Lily grinned as her friend jumped to feed her dragon. She wasn't going to be one of those kin who didn't like to share, especially when it made Kellen so happy. Instead, Lily kept a careful eye on the silent conversation passing between Afran and his kin.

Karis finally looked her way, eyes interested. "So Oceana can likely communicate with anyone who is in water—but we can't all communicate with her."

Lily nodded slowly. "Only dragons. And me."

"Well, for now, we're only certain of you and Kis."

Right. Because all the other dragons hated water. Then Lily remembered. "And Fendellen. Oceana could understand her, at least some, even without water."

Karis glanced at Afran and nodded. "She comes into her powers early. Dragon queens can speak mind-to-mind with anyone, but Fendellen is stronger than most queens already."

Lily made a face. The Dragon Star should have picked Fendellen instead of a dragon who apparently only wanted to send impertinent thoughts to everyone and ignore their replies.

Afran rumbled and looked at the blue-green dragon currently nose-deep in a fruit pastry. ::Perhaps Fendellen should teach the next fire lessons.::

Karis raised an eyebrow. "It's a thought. She did teach Lotus how to fly."

Lily grimaced. Fendellen had done the final flying lesson, but Sapphire and Lotus had done a lot of work before that. Hard, dusty, bruising work. "I'll take Oceana to see Kis today."

Karis chuckled. "I'll warn Irin."

Kellen and Lily cringed together.

::I'll warn Irin.:: Afran sounded amused this time. ::He was not pleased about fire in his nursery, but he will allow the lessons.::

Lily tilted her head at him, hearing an odd note in the dragon's words.

It was Karis who provided the answer. "He's pleased that his dragon has found a reason to wake up in the mornings." She smiled over at Kellen. "Kis just sent for a second bowl of breakfast stew."

That was a very big deal—for Kis, who often didn't eat enough to keep his moods pleasant, and for Kellen, who had cooked the stew.

Lily set down her half-eaten bread and got up. Time to tell a small dragon that she might have won part of this battle, but she wasn't going to win the war. If facing their biggest fear was what she and Oceana had to do, she needed to make sure one cheeky dragon did the work. It was time to go make their skin itch.

CHAPTER 14

*L*ily took a running leap and pulled her knees up to her chest, landing in a ball and spraying water everywhere. She laughed as Alonia splatted into the warm pool right beside her. Then they both cleared out of the way, because Sapphire and Kellen were already leaping.

The antics of elves finally free from lessons and chores and fire training. Lily looked around long enough to spy her dragon sitting on her sunning rock and eyeing all of them with astonishment. Lily had played in the pool with Oceana before, but apparently four wet elves were a shock.

Alonia came up behind her. "Maybe she doesn't like being splashed."

Lily snorted. When it came to splashing, her dragon gave as good as she got. She flicked a light spray Oceana's way. "Come and play, silly creature."

The vague impression she got before a blue-green streak launched off the rock was one of absolute glee. Lily didn't bother warning her friends. Elves weren't like dragons, especially her closest friends. None of them were fragile around water. Not since they'd built the pool, anyway. She ducked under the water, looking for her dragon, and heard Alonia's surprised screech.

She surfaced just in time to see Kellen fall over laughing. Alonia picked Oceana up and glared at her, nose to nose. "Not funny."

"It totally was." Sapphire cackled and tipped herself sideways, splashing everyone in the pool. "You looked like one of those fish statues in your cousin's garden."

"Oh, sure." Alonia sounded more amused than annoyed. "Just wait until she tries to squirt water into your mouth."

Sapphire wasn't done laughing. "I guess next time you'll close yours instead of leaving it flapping in the wind."

"I was trying to breathe," Alonia said, angling Oceana in Sapphire's direction. Lily grinned as her dragon happily cooperated and thunked her tail down on the surface of the water.

Kellen ducked under the spray, giggling. "No fair using a dragon as a weapon."

Lily snorted as Oceana's tail struck again. "She's my dragon. She should get to be my weapon."

"Finders, keepers." Alonia winked at Oceana, tossed her high in the air, and got out of the way. Which wasn't necessary. Blue-green wings unfurled and one small dragon pushed herself skyward—and then turned around and folded her wings, plummeting back toward the pool like a dropped boulder.

Alonia gasped, which was a bad move, because it meant her mouth was open when Oceana hit the water. Lily managed to keep hers closed and dove under, picking up her feet so she could ride the wave of her dragon's cannonball.

When she surfaced, the water level in the pool was a lot lower. Lily felt the much-colder water of the river behind her seeping in through the rock wall. She glared at her dragon, mostly in jest. "Keep that up and we'll have to go find a dragon to heat up the water again."

Oceana chittered happily and sent a picture of Kis.

Lily rolled her eyes. "If any of the rest of us woke him up as much as you do, we'd be turned into elf stew. He's not about to leave his nice, comfortable bed just because you splashed too much water out of the pool."

"He might." Alonia laughed. "He likes Oceana. He only tolerates the rest of us."

There was a lot of truth to that. Lily felt another cold finger of water reach her from the river, and dove under. There was more than one way to stay warm. Time to teach her friends the fine art of finding a dragon tail in the water.

By the time they pulled themselves out onto the sunning rocks, dripping wet and cold and having swallowed half the pool, the sun had worked its way much farther down in the sky, and Lily was as happy as she'd been in a long time. She ran a finger over her dragon's very content, very droopy spikes. She swallowed, trying hard not to be sad at what would come next.

"What's wrong?" Alonia frowned a little as she wrung the water out of her hair.

Nothing she wanted to share and spoil the best afternoon in forever. Lily kept her fingers in the water and her other hand on Oceana's spikes. "It's nothing."

Sapphire snorted and hit her in the back of the head with the old cloth she was using to dry off.

Lily sighed. "Oceana feels so real right now. She's all big and bright and strong in our kin bond." She paused, not wanting to speak of the hard thing that had been weighing like a boulder in her chest since the first moment she'd felt her dragon. "She doesn't usually feel like that."

More like a shadow. Or a dragon ghost.

"It's because we played with her." Kellen's voice was quiet, but she sounded unusually certain. "Oceana isn't a baby, but she never really got to be one. She was alone all that time. She didn't get to be silly with her friends, and I think she needs that. We learn by having fun together. Irin plays with the baby dragons too, even if he won't admit it."

Lily had seen that often enough. "Even Kis does. He pretends he's thumping his tail in his sleep so they can chase it."

Kellen nodded vigorously. "Exactly. If you make things too hard for a baby dragon, they quit. Or they fall asleep."

That described Oceana exactly. "So we need to help her bond to us and to the dragons by playing together?" It made a lot of sense—until Lily tried to imagine Afran playing a game of tag.

"I think you're right," Sapphire said quietly. "You have to tell Karis. Or Irin."

Kellen shook her head.

Lily swallowed hard. "Then I will, because if you're

right, trying to teach Oceana to be brave around fire is exactly the wrong lesson. She might quit or turn into a ghost or nap all day." Things Oceana knew how to do really well, because being alone for a hundred years or more would have been the hardest of hard.

Alonia nodded slowly. "Like Kis."

Lily stared. It was exactly like Kis. When he tried to sleep all day, they took turns going to sing to him and bringing his favorite foods and asking him to tell stories. Not playing, but making sure he had lots of reasons to keep opening his eyes.

A throat cleared behind them. "What's like Kis?"

Lily scrambled to her feet, staring at Karis and Irin.

Karis looked at Sapphire. "Lotus told Afran you wanted to see us."

"I told Lotus to send the message." Sapphire glared back at Lily's dirty look. "You're marked by the Dragon Star, just like I am. That means what Kellen said is important. If we're trying to teach Oceana the wrong lessons, they need to know."

Lily swallowed hard. She didn't like that explanation at all, but she couldn't say it was wrong.

"Sounds like an interesting discussion." Irin took a seat on a rock and cast Lily a calm glance. "Tell us how you think Oceana needs to be taught."

Lily's throat felt like she was swimming underwater and desperate for air. "I think Kellen should explain it." She looked over at her friend and tried to put as much apology and pride as she could into her eyes. "It's her idea, and I think she's right, and she can explain it the best."

Kellen just squeaked.

Irin picked up a small stick and twirled it between his fingers. "I'm not surprised. Kellen has more sense than any three other elves I know."

Kellen's squeak this time was a lot more surprised.

Irin raised an eyebrow at her. "If you have something to say, missy, we're both smart enough to listen."

"It's mostly about Karis." Kellen was almost whispering. She gulped and looked at Karis. "And Afran."

Karis's lips twitched. "Speak, youngling. Neither Afran nor I are so fragile that we can't handle a few critical words."

"It's not criticism, exactly." Kellen's words came out as a whoosh. "We all have things we do really well, but sometimes we can get stuck in them."

Karis nodded solemnly. "That sounds like a wise observation."

Kellen's voice steadied a little. "I'm small and feisty and I'm really good at being patient, but sometimes I can be patient for too long and not speak up when something's wrong." She took a deep breath. "You and Afran are really wise and good at figuring out what lessons we need to learn, but you stick to those ideas for a long time. Which helps us to learn hard things, but—" She broke off, twisting her fingers in her tunic.

Karis reached out and tipped up her chin. "But sometimes we stick to ideas that might be wrong. You think we might be doing that this time."

Kellen looked almost ready to cry. "Maybe."

An enormous dragon nose moved in and whiffed air on Kellen's cheek. ::To speak such words to those you respect takes enormous courage, youngling.::

Lily swallowed, really grateful for her friend's brave words and that Karis and Afran had been able to hear them.

Kellen sat down abruptly, clearly realizing what she had just done.

Karis laughed. "Oh no, my small and feisty student. You don't get out of this that easily. You've told us we're holding too tightly to the wrong ideas. Now you need to tell us the idea you've kept quiet about, perhaps for too long."

Kellen's cheeks flushed even more pink. "I don't have much of one. Just that we need to play, exactly like we did today."

Lily had a quick mental vision of a bunch of dragons splashing around in her pool like half-grown elves and laughed. That surely wouldn't work.

And then she felt the wave of need smash into her. Oceana, picking up her silly idea through the water that connected them both. Seeing the dragons in the water. Wanting. Desperately, frantically yearning for that to be real.

Oh, no. Lily reached for her dragon, arms out, heart cracking. "It can't happen. The dragons are too scared of the water." She was already cursing herself for what had been a light joke in her head. "We'll find a way for you to play together, but it can't be that."

"I'm not so sure." Irin's gruff voice sounded surprised—astonished, even. And more than a little alarmed. "I have a dragon in my head who doesn't agree with you."

Lily just stared at him.

Karis found her words first. "You think we should ask the dragons to go *swimming*?"

Irin swayed a little, looking totally poleaxed. "I don't. But the old man does."

Kis. Lily hissed in a breath. It would never work. Ever. "He's the only one who can even put his tail in."

"I know." Irin nodded, and his back straightened. "Kis says this will be hard, but that Kellen is correct. We were asking hard of the wrong dragons."

Karis was looking at Irin like he'd grown soup greens out his ears. "We can't ask the dragons to go swimming."

Irin's lips turned up in a faint smile. "We won't have to." Eyes flashing with pride, he turned his head toward the village. "He will."

Lily stared—and then a great dragon bugle rang out into the night, bouncing off her ears and all the way up to the sky.

Karis sucked in a single shocked breath. "A challenge? Is he mad?"

Lily felt her stomach drop into her feet. She knew what that was, even though she'd never heard one. A formal dragon call to arms. A cry that had not rung for more than ten generations. And one that no self-respecting dragon would be able to ignore.

Kis had just called all of dragonkind into battle.

INTERLUDE

Lovissa woke, shuddering and cold and taking far longer than a warrior should to realize that the elf-infested water had not touched her scales.

A dream. A true one, a vision of the time that would come in some forsaken land where dragons and elves shared the bond of kin.

She shook the visceral disgust off her skin. She had seen the dreams for an entire winter, and the prophecy was clear. One day, not all dragons would feel as she felt.

Amusement filtered through the less-pleasant feelings. At least the dragons to come still retained the proper attitude toward water. She puffed out air slowly into a morning not yet warmed by the sun. The old yellow warrior had been a frequent visitor in her dreams, and he had earned her respect. His injuries, scarred and grievous, would have made him a hero in her time.

But even old heroes could take wrong steps. Damaged warriors, seeking the glory of battle one more time.

She snorted. Respectfully. This time, the yellow dragon had

INTERLUDE

picked the wrong enemy. Water could not be vanquished. It must simply be avoided. Even the arrival of a dragon so strange as the blue-green one did not have the power to alter such a fundamental truth.

She bowed her head. His call to battle had been magnificent, stirring up her blood even as she slept. She could feel the power of it, pushing against her scales from the inside. No dragon living could fail to be moved by such a summons. Even her old and tired wings yearned to rise and join with such might.

She snorted again, this time at herself, and tucked her head back onto her tail. It was early yet, the first light of the sun not yet fully chasing away the dark, and smart dragons with spring campaigns to plan needed to get their rest. The yellow warrior lived in a time and place far removed from the Veld. It would be others who must respond—and gently turn his fierce heart to wiser battles.

He had a good queen. She had both age and wisdom. She would know what to do with an old warrior who had lost his way.

Lovissa tried once again to settle. This dream had been uncommonly disturbing. She rolled a little, her shoulder aching from old battle wounds. Always, the ache was worse in the winter, but she did not wish the pain away, for that would mean spring had come, and danger along with it.

She closed her eyes. A warrior must sleep when she could.

An enormous roar sounded in the valley outside her cave.

Lovissa was on her feet in a single beat of her heart, ready to throw body and soul into protecting the Veld. She made it as far as the mouth of her cave, preparing her own call to add to the alert—and then the message in Baraken's roar landed in her sleep-fogged head.

INTERLUDE

She froze on the cliff's edge, gaping at the utter silence below.

There was no danger to the Veld. No elf invasion. Baraken was not sending a battle cry—he was answering *one. The one that had sounded in her dream.*

The one calling all dragons to the water.

-oOo-

Lovissa spotted her quarry and angled for the cliffs below. It wasn't the first place she had thought to look, but Baraken's large bulk wasn't hard to find.

He gave her a hard look as she glided in for a landing, but queens were made of sterner stuff than to melt under a warrior's glare, even a warrior as fine as this one. She flapped her wings in the movements that would have once landed her as gently as a flower blossom touching down on a meadow of grass. These days, she felt fortunate if the thunk wasn't overly jarring. She did not let the lack of grace embarrass her. All flyers eventually lost their skill to age—and in its place, gained wisdom.

She was here to see whether it was age and wisdom that chased her finest warrior, or something else. She had reason to be concerned. He had been bellowing all through the night, roaring his answer to the challenge in her dreams. It had woken half the Veld, and not the half that tended toward reasoned and temperate behavior.

She folded her wings neatly on her back and stared out over the choppy gray water. Not a dragon's usual choice of views. "We must speak."

He stared down at the water far below, at the line where it met the sands that were all that remained of what had once been proud cliffs. It reminded Lovissa oddly of the ashes of the queens.

She waited. He was not always quick to speak, but it was generally worth the wait.

His rumble formed into words. "I must go to the water. Touch it."

Cold struck her bones. His words edged far too close to her dream. "Why?"

"I do not know." He blew smoke down at the waves encroaching on the beach. "The summons is clear."

She had heard it, but it had not been calling to her. Perhaps it had not been calling to him either. "I have dreamed of this. It comes from the dragons who will come after us." She moved her head a little closer to his, the most a queen dared in trying to soothe a warrior. "It is not our challenge, Baraken. It is for those who will come from us."

She wasn't sure she believed the words even as she spoke them. It was one thing for a queen to receive the visions. It was entirely different for her finest warrior to have seen them too.

"It is for me." He sounded absolutely certain, even as a shudder moved over his body.

She knew why. Water was an enemy second only to the elves, and often used by them. An aversion at the deepest levels of instinct, made stronger by experience. "Perhaps you need only to be close."

His wings unfurled. "No. I must touch the water."

Unease gripped her throat. "For how long?"

His shoulders rippled. "I do not know."

That wasn't acceptable. She needed him. Some skirmishes had already been fought, and the major campaigns of spring needed planning. She needed his skill and his might and his rock-solid certainty that they would win.

Baraken of the cliffs did not feel certain of anything, and it unsettled her greatly. "Come back with me. We need to calm the youngsters you've woken with your bellowing. They think we march on the elves today."

"You will calm them. They will listen to their queen. I must stay here."

On that, his certainty felt absolute. A warrior who would not be swayed, even if his cause was a wrong-headed one.

Lovissa sighed. The planning of the spring campaigns could wait a day or two, but no more. The snow in the passes melted early this year. "I will send one of our fastest flyers if we require your presence." No warrior of the Veld ever truly got to stand down.

He nodded. "That is acceptable."

It wasn't his choice. She was his queen. She would have some of their scouts check on him. He would not be the first warrior to get cracked in the head. Battle broke many things, and not all of them were visible.

She unfurled her own wings. The battle with the water was one he must fight alone.

She had dragons to ready for spring.

PART III
VOICES FROM AFAR

CHAPTER 15

Trin looked up from his work at a high table as Lily and Oceana entered the nursery. "About time you two showed up."

Lily blinked, and then blinked again as a very alert golden eye scanned her. It was still early, and Kis was rarely awake before midday. "I'm sorry—did you send for us? I didn't get the message." After a dawn swim, she'd decided to bring her hungry dragon into the village for breakfast. Kellen was on kitchen duty this morning, and she wouldn't threaten Oceana with a ladle for coming too near the soup pot.

"I sent for you," said a voice behind her. Karis walked in with a very drowsy Sapphire and an even sleepier Lotus. The peach-pink dragon headed straight for a nook beside Kis, turned herself around once to get settled, and promptly fell back asleep. Karis shook her head at the young dragon and nodded briskly at Lily. "We went by your pool to pick you up, but evidently you're early risers this morning."

Lily took a seat on a low stool. "We didn't sleep much. Too many dragons flying overhead."

"Indeed." Karis cast a wry glance at Kis's visible eye. "Care to explain yourself to mere elves, old man? I assume you don't actually intend to lead a flight of dragons off to war."

Irin snorted and stabbed a piece of cheese with a small knife. "Is that what your dragon told you?"

Karis raised an eyebrow. "No. Afran is being uncharacteristically silent."

Irin folded his arms and stared at his dragon. "Indeed."

Lily and Sapphire exchanged glances. This didn't bode well. Lily had no idea what was going on either. Kin bonding with a dragon was supposed to let you in on most of the dragon chatter, but if even Karis and Irin didn't know what was happening, this was a very strange morning.

And a scary one. Lily shivered, and it wasn't from the cold. The nursery was always the warmest place in the village.

Karis gave her a small nod. Then she took the bread and cheese Irin offered and pinned Kis with a stern gaze. "Enough with the mystery. Explain your challenge, please. We're kin, and leaving us in the dark is going to turn this thing into a cock-eyed mess."

::Kin are not a part of this.:: Kis sounded clear and stern and a lot less cranky than he usually did. ::It is dragons who have erred, and dragons who must fix this.::

Karis and Irin both looked ready to pound on something. Irin growled. "Explain, old man."

The golden eye didn't move, didn't blink—but something in its depths gentled. The eye shifted to look straight at Lily. ::You worry that your bond with your dragon is not strong enough. I believe you are wrong in that:: His eye shifted to include the others. ::There is a bond that is far too weak, however, and it is the one that runs from the small blue-green one to other dragons.::

Kis stopped talking, as if they were smart enough to figure the rest out.

Lily swallowed, her head feeling like she'd drunk too much mead.

It was Irin who blew out a sharp exhale. "Warriors fight best when they know who they fight for."

::Exactly. The small one is marked of the Dragon Star, and yet she feels like an outsider. This must not be allowed to continue. She will one day be called to save all of dragon kind. To do that, she must know us, or she will have no reason to take to dangerous skies.::

Like Kis had done once. Lily's stomach clenched.

Kis's eye gentled again. ::I do not speak of literal skies, missy. I do not believe it will be arrows you face.::

Lily wasn't sure they were capable of facing much of anything.

Kis's eye moved to Oceana, who had wrapped herself around Irin's warm mug of cider. ::She lives in a fog, one born out of years of solitude. The only ones to have made it through that fog have come to join her in the water.::

Lily thought of Oceana's glee as Kellen, Sapphire, and Alonia had jumped in the pool. And of her pleasure when

Kis had laid down at the water's edge and communed with her, the tip of his tail in the water.

Kis rumbled. ::She must know us. We have failed in leaving the task for forming that bond in her hands.::

"We've been working on it," Karis said quietly.

::You have not been working correctly. You have been asking the small one to come out of her fog instead of seeking to understand it.::

Lily winced at the hard words. Karis merely frowned.

::There has not been enough respect.:: Kis paused, and the nursery reverberated with his sternness. ::Especially from the dragons. We laugh when the small one hisses when we make fire. We do not honor the chosen of the Dragon Star. We must begin. We must ask her to wrap her fog around all of us.::

He gingerly guided the very tip of his tail into Irin's cider. ::We will come join you in the water, small one. We will swim.::

The force of his promise reverberated in Lily's bones.

Irin eyed his cider and raised a wry eyebrow. "I'm thinking a dare would have gotten the job done, old man. Did you really need to issue a battle challenge?"

::Yes.:: Kis looked exactly like Lily imagined a dragon warrior would look—and not an old and cranky one. ::They are marked of the Dragon Star. I take this as seriously as any battle of my lifetime.::

Shock hit Irin's face. "You're making sure they all come. Every dragon. All those able to travel."

Kis merely blinked. ::Indeed.::

Irin snorted. "You're crazy."

::No. I am the warrior who will be first into the water.::

Kis raised his head and looked straight at Lily. ::Please ask Kellen to fetch me some of her stew for breakfast. There are preparations to make. We must begin.::

Lily was still stuck on what Irin had said. "All the dragons will come?"

Kis blinked slowly. ::Of course. They will not ignore my summons.::

Lily gulped. There would be hundreds of dragons. Most wouldn't fit in the warm pool all by themselves, and even the river could only hold a handful at a time. "I don't think there's enough room."

Kis's rumble sounded amused. ::We will go to the bay of a thousand waterfalls. There will be room for us all.::

Lily blinked. She'd been there twice. It was a beautiful ocean bay fed by springs and water cascading down from the cliffs, but it was at least three days away by foot, maybe more. Kis could hardly make it to the sunning rocks. She swallowed and found the courage to look straight into his eyes. ::That's really far away.::

::I will be leaving directly after breakfast.:: Kis's head rose right to the ceiling of the rondo. ::In fact, I believe I will eat my stew outside.::

Lily scrambled out of the way as three dragons of very different sizes headed for the doors, four astonished kin following in their wake. Karis looked at Irin on the way out and shrugged wordlessly. Irin grabbed a canteen and a knife and a pack from the corner. "I go where he goes."

That seemed to spur Karis out of her shock. "I'll go organize supplies. Walk with what you absolutely need. We'll ferry the rest."

Afran could fly to the bay, and so could Lotus. Lily

sighed as she exited the nursery, realizing she only had one way of getting there. One that involved a lot of dust and a very cranky dragon. She looked over at Oceana, who had found a perch on a nearby rain barrel. Maybe she could be convinced to fly with Lotus and Sapphire while those who had to walk marched through the dust.

Karis waved Sapphire off. "Go wake everyone."

That was going to be a lot of people, and not all of them had dragons to ride. Kellen would probably walk without complaint, but Alonia was *not* going to be happy about this. Except for the part where every single dragon within three days' travel was going to be there. Lily hid a sudden grin. She was pretty sure matchmaking wasn't part of what Kis was trying to do, but Alonia never waited for permission. Not if there were cute boys or dragons in the vicinity.

Irin slapped his hand to Kis's shoulder. "Eat your stew, fearsome warrior, and we'll see if we can talk someone into flying our gear to where we'll overnight so I don't have to lug your dinner."

Lily winced—she knew exactly how much a small dragon could eat. Feeding Kis on the trail was going to be a logistical nightmare.

"We'll sort it out." Karis straightened from her conversation with a newly arrived Alonia, who looked uncommonly serious. "You go. We'll get the gear ready, recruit a few of Lotus's friends to be our supply train, and we'll be on the trail after you by mid-morning."

Lily cast a surreptitious glance in Kis's direction. At any speed she'd ever seen the old dragon walk, even the slowest travelers would catch up to him by lunch.

Alonia walked over and rubbed Kis's nose. "I'll forage

for berries along the way. The first ones should be ripe by now."

That was a really excellent bribe, especially if Kellen could be convinced to toss them into some trail pancakes, but food wasn't going to get Kis through this journey. Lily didn't doubt his courage, but his body barely worked these days.

She shook her head. Irin didn't look worried, and Kis wasn't who she should be fussing over. The journey would be hard, but others would lead—and if Irin couldn't get Kis there, no one could. It was the destination Lily needed to worry about. Several hundred dragons who hated water were not exactly ideal candidates for a swimming lesson, and she was pretty sure she knew who the swimming teachers were supposed to be. She let out a sigh, and then clapped her hand over her mouth, realizing it had been a really noisy one.

Irin glanced in her direction. "You worry about getting yourself on that trail, missy. Kis and I have never been left behind on a march, and we won't be starting now."

Lily felt her cheeks flushing. She hadn't meant for her doubt to be so obvious. "I'm worried about the swimming, too."

"Worries are eased by doing, youngling."

Lily looked over at the unfamiliar voice—and stared. Elhen, queen of the dragons and so old she was almost transparent, stood beside the nursery rondo with her two guardians at her back.

The village had gone absolutely silent.

Elhen surveyed the frozen people, the half-gathered supplies, and the golden dragon at the center of all the action. A wave of amusement reverberated in Lily's head. "You called, old man?"

Kis looked almost sheepish. "It was not necessary for the queen to answer."

Elhen snorted. "There has been only one battle cry sounded in my lifetime. I wasn't going to stay in my cave and eat strawberries."

Kis dropped his head. "I follow where you lead."

This time, Elhen's mental merriment jangled like bells. "Oh, no, old man. You started this one. You lead." She paused a beat. "You have issued a challenge for all of dragonkind—and I believe you have issued it correctly. Our past and our future may well rest on how many of our number can meet your bravery."

Lily could have sworn Kis was turning pink under his golden scales.

Elhen turned her head and sought out Kellen, who stood awed and still, a loaf of bread in one hand and a pot of stew in the other. "I have heard rumors of your wondrous stew, young Kellen. Perhaps I might trouble you to bring me a bowl."

Kellen held up the pot and tried to say something that mostly came out as a stutter.

Elhen's eyes twinkled. "Three bowls, if you please." Without even a pause, the queen daintily dipped her tail in the rain barrel where Oceana perched. Lily didn't hear what was said, but from the stunned, shy look on her dragon's face, she had just been invited to dine with royalty.

CHAPTER 16

*L*ily dropped down on the rocks at the edge of the cliff that overlooked the bay of a thousand waterfalls and moaned in relief. Four days of living hell, but she'd survived. Barely. She glanced overhead as Oceana shot by, Lotus hard on her tail, Sapphire screeching at her dragon to stop.

Lily grinned. Oceana's nosedive would take her straight for the water. Lotus was going to get thoroughly splashed if she wasn't careful.

Moments later, a blue-green streak arrowed into the water, and Lotus blew fire at the splash. Ocean popped up safely out of range, chittering happily.

"Your dragon has a strange sense of humor."

Lily gulped and looked over at the queen, who had taken to speaking to her at odd moments. "She likes to play."

"That would be why we're here," Elhen replied calmly,

turning to look over her shoulder. "What say you, old man? Do we jump from here?"

Lily sprang to her feet, throwing herself between the elderly queen's body and insanity. "No, don't do that." She gulped as a regal eye nearly melted her where she stood. "There's a path down. On the other side. To the sand." She could feel her knees banging together, but no queens were going to die on her watch if she could help it, or old warriors either. Kis and Elhen had both made the long four days of walking entirely without complaint, but every morning as they arose, their bodies had been stiffer. Kis hadn't taken a single step without pain, and the queen, steadfast as her spirit might be, seemed even more translucent than when the journey had begun.

"Don't worry about them," said a new voice, full of humor. "They're tough as mountains, both of them. It's the rest of us you need to worry about."

Lily gaped as Fendellen landed on the cliff beside her, light as a feather.

The queen-to-be bowed to Elhen, and then bowed almost equally deeply to Kis. "You called, old man. I have come."

"Not alone, I imagine," Elhen said crisply.

Fendellen merely turned and folded in her wings to reveal the vista behind her.

Lily looked this time—really looked. The bay was gorgeous, the sun glistening off of salt water which was almost the exact color of Oceana's lightest scales, surrounded by cliffs of beautiful rocks, steep pitches of black and red with glints of gold and streaks of pure white.

Forest crowded almost to the cliff tops, and from the

depths of the trees, spring-fed water flowed, spilling over the cliffs in an uncountable number of waterfalls. Some were tiny, small arrows of falling mist gently raining on the sands and water below. Some fell as great heavy dumps, landing with foam and thunder.

On the top of the cliffs, ringing the bay and carefully keeping their feet on dry rocks, were more dragons than Lily had ever seen.

Elhen surveyed those she ruled. "You have brought more than I expected. Perhaps this is a day for the young to lead."

Crisp smoke blew out Fendellen's nostrils, but it was Kis she answered, not her queen. "This is your battle, old man. I only came to hold your sword while you fight it."

Kis's eyebrow ridges slid up. "I expect you to be the third one in."

Lily gulped. That meant Kis was very sure he and Elhen were going swimming

Fendellen simply nodded. Challenge accepted.

"Well done." Elhen's words conveyed her approval—and her merriment as a blue-green streak darted around Fendellen's head. "I see that she remembers you."

The queen-to-be blew smoke at Oceana's tail. "Are those any kind of manners to show in front of your queen?" She sighed as the small dragon took off, chittering, heading straight for the water. "I believe my job today will be making sure she doesn't splash anyone before they're ready."

Lily winced and dared to speak. "That should probably be my job."

"Probably." Fendellen's eyes sparkled. "But since you

can't fly, why don't you lead the way down the path to the sand, and I'll see if I can keep your menace out of trouble until you can put your fingers in the water and tell her to behave."

After four days of dust, Lily intended to put a lot more of herself in the water than her fingers, but she recognized the honor she had just been given. She hurried to put herself in front of Elhen and Kis. "This way." There was more than one path down, but many were a hard slide even for a nimble elf. The one that would be wide enough for dragons led down to the widest strip of beach and would let them stay far back from the water's edge and Oceana's foolish antics.

Or maybe not so foolish. Lily breathed in the immensity of what was about to happen. All of dragonkind had come to play with her dragon today. That was worth getting excited about.

Assuming any of them actually made it into the water.

Lily refused to think about what might happen if they balked.

Fendellen took off after the small dragon streaking headfirst toward the water. Lily peeled her eyes away—there would be plenty of time to watch Oceana's antics later, and she had a queen and a warrior to guide. She tried to swallow, but four days of travel hadn't left anything in her mouth but dust.

A canteen appeared under her nose. Irin fell in beside Lily, as he'd done several times on the journey. She cast him an unsure look. "If you know a better way down, you should lead."

He chuckled. "Both of the old farts walking behind us

are more than capable of using their wings and gliding down to the beach. They do this to make a point. Half of dragonkind is up on those cliffs. This is theater, nothing more."

Lily managed a blessed swallow of water from the canteen and kept her eyes off the cliffs. The queen at her back was pressure enough. "Gliding would be pretty impressive."

"Not to a bunch of thimble heads who can fly circles around both of them." Irin took back his canteen. "Do your best to look like someone who enjoys pomp and circumstance so we can do the old farts proud."

A blast of hot air hit her back. ::Our hearing is not as elderly as you seem to think.::

Lily gulped. Elhen didn't sound mad, but it couldn't be a good thing to insult the queen.

::And you misunderstand our intent. This is not a procession.::

Kis raised an eyebrow. "Fine. Dusty and tired it is, then."

Lily was entirely lost. Dusty and tired was the exact opposite of pomp and circumstance. "I don't understand—they want to look weak?"

Irin chuckled. "Only if the fools up on the cliffs ate their common sense for breakfast."

She definitely didn't understand.

It was Elhen who explained. ::A good warrior shows their strength. A great warrior waits to show it until exactly the right moment.::

Lily slipped on a rock covered in loose dirt and cursed. Even a hare-brained warrior didn't pick a clumsy elf for an escort. She focused on finding the path down, guiding the dragons at her back into the scrubby bushes through the widest opening she could find. Irin made a sound that might be approval.

Carefully, no longer worried about anything other than getting them all down to the bay in one piece, Lily picked her way through the twists and turns of a path that was not human or elf made, but clearly not intended for dragon travel either. She slowed, knowing they neared the steepest part of the descent, and felt a hot puff of smoke on her back. She scurried forward, Irin casually hopping boulders and bush limbs beside her. She wondered if he was making a point to the onlookers too.

When she finally stepped onto warm, dry sand, Lily let out a breath that could probably be heard up on the cliffs. She turned, nodded once at Kis and Elhen, and stepped out of the way. This part was definitely not her show.

Four wings flared as one, queen and warrior standing wingtip to wingtip, their necks arching to catch the rays of the midday sun. A roar rose from the cliffs. Lily couldn't her own quiet gasp. Even dust-covered and weary, Elhen and Kis were magnificent.

Great warriors know when to show their strength.

Oceana buzzed by in the air, scattering droplets of water everywhere. Lily hissed, trying to get her dragon's attention. Elhen merely stood as water sprayed across her nose. The wildly excited blue-green dragon headed straight for the water and dove in, surfacing with her eyes full of invitation.

Elhen looked at Kis and nodded regally. "After you, old man."

With no hesitation at all, Kis walked straight to the water's edge and in. He didn't stop until the waves lapped halfway up his forelegs.

Oceana abruptly calmed, swimming in quiet circles, eyes glued to whatever he was telling her through the water.

Lily's heart filled.

Kis raised his head, eyes still on Oceana, his voice ringing out over the bay and up the cliffs to waiting dragon ears. "Our weakness was believing that you needed to become more like us, small one. That you needed to learn to let go of your water and stand in our fire. In that, we have erred. Today, I ask to stand in your water."

Lily could feel her stomach literally trying to rise up through her throat. She took the two steps to the water's edge and dropped her fingers into the sea, overwhelmed by Kis's honesty and bravery—and laughed out loud as she discovered that Oceana wasn't overwhelmed at all.

The small dragon was entirely focused on her friend, chittered happily, calling him deeper into the water. Ignoring the hordes on the cliffs, almost as if they didn't exist.

Lily frowned. That wasn't good.

Kis met her eyes. ::That is not your worry for today, missy. It is ours.::

::Indeed.:: Elhen had stepped to the water's edge. She hesitated the tiniest moment and delicately dipped her front claws in the bay. ::May I come swim in your waters, little one?::

From the loud, nervous rumbling on the cliffs, Lily surmised all in attendance had heard the queen's request.

Elhen nodded at Oceana, who sent back only wordless, incandescent glee, and raised her own head high. "We do this for the dragons of old, for the dragons of now, and for all those who will come from our lines. And we do it because it is not right for any of us to stand alone." She took two more steps into the water.

Lily gaped as the queen of all dragonkind lifted her tail slowly and solemnly—and slapped it down on the water, raining splatters all over the golden dragon beside her.

Kis roared, nearly jumping out of his skin—and dove, straight into the deep of the bay. Elhen blew out a stream of fire and followed him.

Lily stood on the shore, dumbfounded, as two of dragonkind's oldest and most regal members cavorted in the water like children. Chasing each other. Splashing. Trapping Oceana between them and utterly soaking her, much to the small dragon's delight.

Then Kis raised his head, looked straight at the stunned dragons assembled on the cliffs overhead, and roared his challenge again.

CHAPTER 17

Mass confusion broke out on the cliffs. Dragons squirmed and wriggled, and a brave few launched off the cliffs, circling high above the bay. One ungainly dragon tripped over a neighboring claw, nearly pitching into a waterfall and launching himself into the air instead with a panicked screech and enough fire to put the trees below him at serious risk.

::No fire.:: Fendellen's words rang inside Lily's head. ::Our queen and our greatest warrior have shown the way. Let's see if we can manage to follow them without burning down half the forest, shall we?::

Dragon heads dipped, chagrined—but no more left the cliffs to take to the air. And none of those in the air had come any closer to the water.

Lily tried to take a breath. Two dragons had gone into the water. Oceana had been acknowledged as important and worthy. It was not a disaster, even if not a single other dragon managed to go for a swim. But she could feel her dragon's yearning. Her desire for playmates. Her uncertain joy.

A dragon willing to come out of the emptiness permanently—if only the others would meet her there.

She walked into the water, needing to offer Oceana support. Solace.

Her dragon swam in enthusiastic, but increasingly confused circles, casting longing glances at the shore. Elhen and Kis lumbered into the shallows, flanking the beach, small waves lapping at their feet.

Warrior and queen. Waiting.

Just beyond Kis, Irin sat on the shore, eating a bread roll and looking entirely like a man doing nothing more than taking in a day of sun and sand. Lily took a breath and tried to match his casual composure and his clear, understated faith in his dragon and hers.

It was the rest of the dragons she wasn't sure of.

A number were making their way down the path to the beach. Fendellen had led a few others down in graceful flight. Most hadn't left their perches on the cliffs, and the nervous rumbles hadn't stopped since their queen had entered the water.

Now it was the turn of their queen-to-be.

Lily met Fendellen's gaze, and in it, she saw bravery—and something that looked awfully like Alonia right before she did something silly.

The ice-blue dragon turned to the reigning queen and bowed. She did the same to Kis, who snorted. "Get on with it, missy."

::I will, but I intend to do this in a way that those gathered behind me can follow—and perhaps those cowering up on the cliffs as well.::

Lily wasn't sure who was hearing Fendellen's words, but she suspected it included very few dragons. Irin winked at her, still chewing on his bread roll and hid a grin behind his hand. Whatever was coming, he seemed to think it would be worth watching.

Fendellen spread her wings and arched, preening, letting her scales catch the sun. Then she trumpeted into the sky. ::Lotus, my daredevil friend, where are you? I require your assistance.::

A peach-pink body launched off a cliff, making startled chittering sounds as she flew, a very surprised Sapphire clinging to her back.

Fendellen took to the skies in a single flap of her wings. She came alongside Lotus, and together, they circled around fast and tight behind the dragons high up on the rocks. They fired over their heads in formation, an ice-blue streak and a peach-pink one, Sapphire flattened down on her dragon's neck yelling something that might be a curse or a prayer.

Then Lotus moved into the lead and dove straight for the deepest part of the bay, wings pulled in tight to her body.

Lily gaped. Fendellen was supposed to be the next dragon in, but Lotus was on a collision course with the water, the queen-to-be hot on her tail. Two dragon cannonballs, incoming.

At the very last moment, Lotus snapped out her wings, hurtling out to sea with her belly barely a finger's breadth away from the water. Fendellen's wings stayed tucked in as she arrowed into the water—and sent up a splash that soaked everyone in the water and thoroughly splattered those waiting on the beach. Lily ducked as several streams of surprised fire shot over her head, along with bellows and screeches and general dragon cacophony.

::Be still.:: Elhen glared at the protesting dragons on the sand. ::The greatest warrior I have ever known has called us to the water. Do not embarrass your queen.::

Heads hung in shame.

::Better.:: Elhen turned and nodded at Fendellen, who had quietly surfaced in the middle of the bay. ::That's one way to get in.::

Lily hid a grin of her own. Oceana thought it was an entirely splendid entry, which any dragon touching the water could surely feel.

Fendellen did a watery barrel roll and blew smoke at Lotus and Sapphire, circling in the sky. ::You two coming in?::

Lotus promptly executed a barrel roll of her own and dumped Sapphire into the drink. She came up, spluttering, and pointed a finger at her dragon. "No more milk curds for you, missy."

Lily knew that was an entirely empty threat, but Lotus wasn't so sure. She circled closer to the water, making concerned chittering sounds.

Oceana thumped her tail on the water and splashed a peach-pink face.

Fendellen, who had swum into the shallows, stood and extended her wings. ::Follow me, little friend. You can be the next one in.::

Lily wasn't sure whether Lotus had been chosen for

that high honor because of her bravery or her tendency to act before she engaged her brain, but whichever it was, Sapphire's dragon shot off into the sky after the queen-to-be.

Fendellen climbed, spiraling over cliffs and beach, and sounded a loud, triumphant reply to Kis's roar.

Dragons rose up, dozens of them responding, as if her call was attached to their wings.

Lily immediately saw what the ice-blue dragon intended and grasped the problem, even if the powerfully flying queen-to-be didn't. That many dragon cannonballs all at once and there wouldn't be a bay left for the last ones to land in. She cupped her hands around her mouth and yelled. "Fendellen! Not all at once!"

There was no chance the dragon flying highest in the sky could hear her.

::Try again. She'll hear you now.:: Elhen sounded like she was ready to fall over giggling.

Lily repeated her words in a more normal tone. If the queen was boosting her words into the sky, there was no need to yell.

Fendellen slowed, high overhead, circling, a dragon horde hot on her tail. ::Sorry—I wasn't thinking. How many?::

Everyone in the water was a good swimmer—or big enough to fend for themselves. Lily held up one hand, thumb tucked in. Dragon hearing might not be all that good, but their vision was impeccable. "Four. No more."

She watched, astonished, as the dragons promptly layered themselves into circling groups of four.

::An old fighting maneuver.:: Kis sounded almost as

entertained as Elhen. ::Apparently, some of them have managed to hold on to their brains.::

One someone hadn't. Lily threw herself after her dragon, who was making a sudden beeline straight for the middle of the bay. Oceana might be the best swimmer, but that didn't mean it was a good idea to be the target for dragon cannonball practice.

::We won't hurt her.:: Fendellen and Lotus, flying highest in the sky, suddenly angled inward and down, dropping through the interior of the circling layers of dragons. Right after them came two more dragons, four sets of wings tucked in tight, faces hurtling into the wind.

Lily screeched and tried to squish herself and Oceana into as small a space as possible, which ended up being on the top of the wave that formed when an ice-blue rock and a peach-pink one hit the water on either side of them. That wave still had them high in the air when two more dragons struck, one blowing fire and the other trying madly to stop and not succeeding.

Lily winced as she toppled off the wild wave. Belly flops hurt, even if you were covered in scales.

Then two more dragons landed, almost on top of the first, and she realized they had bigger problems than awkward landings. She cupped her hands over her mouth again, a whisper yelling into a maelstrom. "Move! Get out of the way!"

The head of every single dragon in the water snapped up and they started swimming with alacrity. Lily stared, not at all sure how they'd even heard her over all the noise. Then she felt Oceana's gently chiding amusement.

She looked over at the wet blue-green head, who was

currently offering up vivid and helpful suggestions on how to swim.

The more water-challenged dragons bellowed their gratitude.

Realization slammed into Lily's heart. Everyone in the water could hear her dragon—and from the impressed gratitude flying her way, they were *glad*.

"Keep them moving." Irin popped up beside them and scratched Oceana's chin. "You're in charge of the idiots, little missy. The smart ones will get out of the way themselves."

Lily laughed as another dragon-sized wave swamped them. This wasn't a swim for the faint of heart. Not that there seemed to be very many of those left. Elves were piling into the water now too, along with a steady rain of dragon cannonballs—and only a couple of the dragons had hastily beat it to shore and gotten back out. Lotus had started a game of tag farther out in the bay, and a number of kin had found their dragons and clambered onto their backs.

When the water finally stopped churning over her head with every other breath, and Oceana only had a couple of dragons who still needed her special brand of mind-to-mind swimming lessons, Lily chanced a look around. Not all of the dragons were in the water. There were still several dozen watchers up on the cliffs, and Afran's great bulk stood on the beach, making no move to get any closer.

::The young and foolish have all gone in.:: Kis, wallowing in the shallows, sounded pleased enough. ::The rest may yet find a more sedate way to enter.::

It didn't matter. It was enough. Lily looked at her

dragon, skimming happily through the water, touching noses with some, daring a small splash at a few others. Beaming happiness in every direction possible. Lily sent Kis a wordless, heartfelt response, one she hoped he could read from this far away. Entirely inadequate thanks for the miracle he had wrought.

One small dragon who belonged.

::He did well.:: Elhen, suddenly swimming at Lily's side, sounded pleased—and very regal. She looked over at the queen-to-be, floating belly-up on Lily's other side. ::As did you. The old man and I sometimes forget to play. That was very well done.::

Fendellen rolled over and tucked in her chin, looking almost self-conscious. Which lasted just long enough for her to lift her tail and send a wave of water straight at Kis. He roared fire at her that was little more than steam and dove under the water, which was a trick very few of the other dragons had found the courage to try yet.

Fendellen had almost made it into the air when she screeched like a young dragonet and suddenly disappeared.

Lily tried not to swallow water as she laughed—and then she felt hands on her ankles, tugging her down into the deep. She twisted her body around to escape and came up, blowing water out her nose and ready to retaliate, expecting one of her friends.

Irin grinned at her. "I grew up near the water elves. You're not the only one who can swim like a fish, missy."

She never would have guessed that in a million years. "Then why don't you ever come to my pool? Or the river?"

The weapons master looked over at his dragon. "Never

wanted to leave him." Irin shook his head as Kis roared more steam and pushed a delighted Oceana under with his tail. "I never figured him for a swimmer."

No one would have—but in the water, Kis's injuries no longer hampered him. "He's having fun."

"He is." Irin sounded proud. "He knew this mattered. He takes the survival of dragonkind very seriously."

Lily gulped, the fun of the day flattening under its true weight. Kis had done this because she and Oceana were marked. Chosen. "I still don't have any idea how we might help with that."

Irin cupped water between his hands and an impressive spout of water shot skyward. "Maybe you've already begun."

Lily looked around the bay full of dragons and elves as silly as she'd ever seen them and felt the giggle rising up her throat. "You think we save the dragons of old by having an enormous water fight?"

Irin snorted as Oceana sluiced water over his head and darted away. "I don't know, missy. But I do know that sometimes the doing of hard things is best accomplished by deepening the bonds of friendship and joy first."

Those were strange words from a man who usually applied a sword to the doing of hard things—but the evidence in the water behind him was unmistakable. Lily gasped as a translucent white tail splashed Kis, and Elhen met a golden-eyed glare with regal innocence.

Which didn't fool Kis at all. Lily giggled madly as the big yellow dragon thoroughly doused his queen. "He's having so much fun."

"We should join him." Irin squeezed her shoulder and

then let go. "First lesson of a warrior. Get food, sleep, and enjoyment while you can. It may not last."

That made her stomach churn. "I don't really know how to do that." To be happy and carry the heaviness all at the same time.

Irin chuckled and ducked as a huge golden tail swung by. "I don't think you're going to get much choice."

Lily spluttered as a great wave of water swooshed over her head and a chittering, gleeful dragon scampered over her shoulder chasing it. She laughed at Oceana's retreating back end. "I'm not a rock, you terrible creature."

Laughing black eyes turned to give her a look and sent a picture of a moss-covered rock with elf ears.

Judging from the amused dragon snorts all over the bay, she wasn't the only one who had seen it. Lily caught a glimpse of Kellen coming up for air and then dipping back down like an otter, swimming just under the surface. Headed straight for Kis's head.

She grinned and sent a quick thought to Oceana. Three could play this game.

CHAPTER 18

Lovissa found a small burst of speed and got herself in front of the frantic scout who had come to fetch her.
::Go. I will speak with him.::

The scout, a battle-hardened veteran not prone to panic, cast her a final distressed glance and angled off sharply. Smart enough to obey his queen. Wise enough to be deeply worried about the dragon on the beach below.

The one who had stood at the water's edge for four days without moving.

Lovissa angled her wings, already complaining about the short, hard flight, and aimed at the sand beside the warrior who had sent a message comprised of a single word.

Come.

She kept her irritation under control. Baraken was a warrior used to giving orders, but even he knew better than to give them to his queen. The circumstances must be dire. She landed hard, spraying sand at water, cliff, and dragon alike. No matter. There were no points for beauty in battle—only survival.

She looked at her fiercest warrior, half a dragon length back from the water and watching it like it would consume all of dragonkind at any moment. Watching and quivering. ::You sent a message. I have come.::

His rumble spoke of a fierce and primal energy, barely constrained. ::I saw them. The ones of the future. The dragons you have seen in your dreams. Swimming in the sea.::

Lovissa's heart nearly stopped. She had spent some of the quiet days of winter sharing portions of her dreams with those of wise minds and strong hearts. ::How do you know this?::

This time, his rumble nearly seared her. ::I saw the old warrior with the wounded wing.:: Baraken's voice was tinged with pride. ::He is of my line.::

Ice and hope collided in Lovissa's breath. ::You can speak to him?::

::I do not know. I only watched.:: A great shudder rolled over Baraken's scales. ::I put a claw into the water, and I saw.::

This was more than even a queen could understand.

Baraken steadied himself. A warrior giving a report. ::There is another. Very small. I believe the small blue-green one makes the seeing possible. She has much power. When she left the water, I could no longer see.::

She had not yet spoken to him of her newest visions. Pride billowed in Lovissa's chest. He was her finest warrior for a reason—his eyes missed nothing. ::She is the second of the five chosen of the Dragon Star.::

Baraken inclined his head.

Her finest warrior had touched his mind to one of the five who would save dragonkind, but that would not leave him shaking like a newly hatched dragonet left out in the cold. ::There was more.::

This time, he turned his head from the waters and blasted her with the fire in his dark green eyes. ::I saw the elves. Many of them. One belongs to the old warrior. Another to the small blue-green one.:: His voice flamed with rage. ::They share a kindred bond. With elves. They have betrayed us.::

Now she understood his fury, and her folly. She had not spoken of the elves in her dreams. Had believed she had time yet before she weakened her warriors in this way. ::Yes. The prophecy speaks thus. There will be five who save us. Five pairs. A dragon and an elf in each pair.::

Something new swam into his eyes. ::You did not tell me.::

Ashes coated her throat. ::We must not rely on the five alone to save us. We must also work to save ourselves.::

He rumbled, his gaze back out over the water. ::We must fight.::

Yes. Fight the ones who would one day save them. She did not understand it any better than he did, but she was queen, and she must think like one. ::Today, we fight. When the time is right, perhaps we will do something different.::

Baraken's fire blasted out over the water, enough to make her eyes itch. ::Perhaps they are not our saviors. Perhaps they are a story planted by our enemies to make us weak. The false tale of the five who will rise up and destroy us.::

::It is not a false tale.::

His roar spoke of a warrior frayed and dangerous. ::The elves have magic. It would be just like their sneaking cowardice to plant such visions.::

Lovissa honored his fire, his rage at those who had stolen far too many of their kindred. Then she waited as he calmed. He must hear the truth. ::The ashes spoke to me of the five. All our queens, speaking as one voice.::

A long silence, Baraken staring out into the water. ::They spoke of the elves?::

She did not let her relief show. ::Yes. They showed me the five. And the elves they name as kin.::

He blew another stream of fire, but this one was not nearly as fierce. ::The peach-pink dragon with the name of a flower, she has an elf?::

Lovissa had shared her midwinter dream of the teenage dragon's flying prowess. She had not shared of the elf riding on her back. ::Yes. She carries an elf into the skies with her.::

Baraken's short roar was as much surprise as horror.

Lovissa stood firm. He must not see how much she wavered inside. Only a queen could hope to lead her dragons into such a terrible new truth, and she would not succeed without her strongest warrior at her side.

One who never failed to give her sage advice. She joined him in staring at the waters, ready to guard against whatever came from the deep. ::We will need to tell the others one day.::

He was silent for so long, she thought he might not answer. ::You are right to keep this hidden. It will weaken them.::

It had already weakened him. She leaned her shoulder gently into his. ::Come. We will go have some food.:: *The first steps of healing were simple ones. She could put his wings and claws on the right path.*

::No.:: *His voice was distant, heading out over the water.* ::I will wait here.::

That way lay madness. ::You will not.::

::I will.:: *Baraken took a single step forward, right to the edge of the cold sea.* ::It is my kin who called the challenge. I will wait. And when it is time, I will touch the water again.::

Lovissa watched, filled with foreboding, as another shudder shivered over his scales. This would not heal her warrior. It might well break him.

Which meant she had only one choice. She wished fiercely for the warmth and comfort of cave and bed and those who would run to do her bidding, and then wrapped her tail around her legs in the sand. ::Then I will wait with you.::

Baraken's rumble cut off mid-breath.

Lovissa let the thought that had surprised him fully form.

::Perhaps it is right that you stay.:: He paused, clearly torn. ::There was a queen standing behind the golden warrior who comes from my line. His queen. She is old, even older than you.::

She snorted. He didn't have to make age sound quite so much like a curse.

His head swayed side to side, still trying to deny. ::She does not have an elf.::

Cold air hissed into Lovissa's chest. She had somehow never considered that a queen might have to share her power with a puny and dangerous enemy. ::No elf will ever rule dragonkind.::

Baraken's rumble was full of deep relief that she was finally speaking sense. ::Perhaps they let only the weak and the foolish join with elves.::

She would not support false stories, even those she fiercely wanted to believe. ::The old warrior of your line has an elf. He is not weak. And the Dragon Star would not choose the weak to save us.::

::It chose a dragon who was scared to fly.:: Baraken's wry tones carried hints of his normal self. ::And one who swims around in water like a fish.::

Sometimes it fell to queens to believe what they could not explain. ::The first flies as well as any dragon in the Veld now.::

Lovissa swallowed and spoke some of the words she had kept hidden through the long, dark winter. ::It was the elf on her back who first got her into the air.:: *The memory of the two of them leaping off the cliffs was one that revisited her frequently while she slept.*

Baraken snorted his surprise.

She had been less surprised. For puny creatures, the elves had always been unexpectedly brave. They died in large numbers because of it.

Her stomach churned. She breathed out slowly and let the warrior beside her see some of her distaste. ::You saw dragons. In the water. Swimming. With elves.::

His look of disgust matched hers. ::Yes. It is not the future I would have wished for.::

It wasn't—except in one respect.

Dragons lived.

CHAPTER 19

Slowly, the dragons in the water were calming. Swimming in. Eyeing their queen, who stood on the shore, water up to her belly, calling her dragons in with nothing but silence.

Lily swam in far enough to feel sand under her feet and stood, waiting. She felt Oceana's tail wrap around her.

Elhen held the silence several heartbeats more. ::We achieved a victory today. We did it for the newest dragon in our midst. We did it to feel our own bravery, and to own our own fear. We did it because one day we will act to save the dragons who came before us, and when that day comes, we will not be weak.::

The dragons rumbled, this time with pride, and contentment.

The sounds of a battle fought and won.

Lily stroked her dragon's chin, thoroughly happy and exhausted. The very best day of her life, coming to an end.

Elhen turned to Kis. ::You called us to the water. What say you, old and brave warrior?::

Kis, who had been playing like the silliest of dragonets all afternoon, looked just as regal as his queen. ::I say the battle is not yet over.:: He paused and looked out over all the dragons, wet and gleaming in the late sun. ::But I say it is well begun.::

Fendellen blew a stream of water high into the air, and those around her who hadn't yet mastered the trick blew fire. Lily giggled as fire and water met and hissed into a fog of steam—and the dragons who had blown them somehow veered off into teams and rallied for one more fight.

Apparently, the day wasn't ending just yet.

-o0o-

The warrior beside Lovissa snapped to attention, his eyes drilling into the water. She waited patiently. This had happened before. Always, he had decided it was not yet time.

He stilled into the hard readiness of a warrior in the moments before a battle was engaged, and she knew this time would be different. She pulled her own readiness into place. Old and tired warrior she might be, but he would not face the monsters of the water alone. Must not face them alone. Because the elves of the water might not be monsters.

They might be salvation.

She stepped forward, a queen ready to do the most important work of her life, and shuddered at the water's edge. Baraken's large shoulder pushed her aside none too gently. "This is warrior work."

She wasn't yet dead, and she would be a warrior until that day, but perhaps he was correct. It was a dragon of his line who had bugled the call.

Baraken dipped a claw in the water, slashed, and pulled it out. Fury rode in his eyes—and also fear. More than she had ever seen there.

A warrior weakened.

It was not for his heart to do battle with this. He had spring campaigns to lead. Lovissa strode forward and placed both her front claws fully in the water. Fierce cold ran up her limbs, aiming straight for her chest, her life, her fire. She held it back by sheer will. Encased herself in a heat that cold could never harm and peered into the water with eyesight and queen sight both.

She gaped at what she saw. Scores of dragons in the water, and amongst them, so many puny dots. Dots with hair and pointy ears. Elves, at least as many as there were dragons.

An enormous bay of water churning with their fighting.

An elf jumped from dragonback onto the head of a dark green dragon who barely had his nose in life-giving air.

Lovissa trumpeted a warning, one that she knew would arrive far too late.

And felt herself knocked out of the water as Baraken charged.

-o0o-

Lily kicked sideways and laughed as Kis swam by, Irin hot on his tail, chasing after a totally unrepentant Fendellen—and felt another presence.

Heard another presence. A loud, nearly deafening roar. A horribly angry one.

Every dragon turned as one toward the mouth of the bay.

"The hell?" Irin popped up beside Lily, on full warrior alert.

Lily shook her head. "I don't know. I feel someone else."

"Dragon." Irin didn't sound at all in doubt. "Kis knows that much."

That didn't make any sense. There were no other dragons in the water.

Oceana sent out a pulse of questioning friendship.

Elhen gasped.

Kis roared.

Irin shot up his dragon's back into riding position, his hand vainly searching for his sword.

Lily dove for her dragon as dozens of large bodies closed ranks in front of them. Fierce Fendellen. Loyal Lotus. Afran guarding the skies above them.

::It is not any dragon of this time.:: Elhen sounded deeply shaken. ::He is a warrior. One who does not recognize me as his queen.::

Lily had a single moment of sheer, blinding panic, and then the other presence, whatever it was, was gone. But she had caught one last horrifying piece of truth, even as her arms had finally wrapped around Oceana.

Fierce, terrible hatred.

CHAPTER 20

*L*ily held her bowl of mostly uneaten stew in her lap. She sat on the shore, her legs still in the water, her dragon's tail wrapped around her waist.

The intruder they could no longer feel still sent shivers through Lily's soul. She had refused to leave Oceana's side, but on the orders of the two dragons currently standing sentinel, all the other elves were staying clear of the waters of the bay. Lily was pretty sure Irin would flout that order in a heartbeat if the hate-filled dragon returned, but for now, Irin walked the sand, on guard and clearly not having any problem eating his stew.

He crouched down at her side and gave a pointed glance at her bowl. "Eat, missy."

She took a small mouthful, knowing better than to argue. She wanted so very much to think only of good things on this day, but much of that had gone up in the smoke of a single blast of hate. "What if that other dragon comes back?"

Irin shrugged. "Then we let Kis and Elhen talk to him. The rest of us will stand ready."

Lily knew what the weapons master meant by those words. "I don't think you can swing a sword at a dragon who lived long ago."

"Maybe not." Irin cupped his hands in the water and looked at Oceana. "But he can't blow fire at us, either. And with your dragon's help, we can talk to him."

Elhen and Kis could, maybe. "I'm not sure he'll talk to an elf." The hate had been bone deep. It still made her skin shiver to think of it, and it had only been a quick flash and gone.

"He's one dragon," Irin said quietly. "If Kis is right, and it's a dragon of his line, then he's likely a fierce and stubborn warrior who is slow to change his mind, but he's still only one dragon."

Lily suddenly felt small and weak and hopelessly insignificant. Even convincing Kis to eat when he was cranky was a monumental task.

"Eat." Irin clapped a hand to her shoulder, nearly pushing her over. "I'm off to make sure Kis does the same, because if that dragon returns, the old man will be the first one trying to stand in front of us."

Lily didn't miss the weapons master's choice of words. "Trying?"

Irin's eyes flashed with something she would never want to mess with. "He might be bigger than me, but he's not tougher. I go where he goes. Always have." He gave her a stern look. "But this is a battle for warriors. Keep your dragon back."

Lily knew darn well he meant for both of them to stay

back. She also knew that wasn't going to be how it worked. "Oceana's not weak." Her elf might be, but that wasn't something Lily could think about right now. "She's the reason we can speak through the water." That half of the Dragon Star's choice no longer seemed like a mistake. "She was chosen for a reason."

Irin raised an eyebrow. "She wasn't chosen alone."

Lily could feel her legs quivering, and it wasn't from the cool water. This day had been full of dragons and elves splashing and playing all around her, but underneath the fun, it had been deadly serious. Something the man in front of her had known days ago—and his dragon, too.

Kis had called them to battle.

Another head descended and eyed her bowl of stew. ::I do hope the small one has eaten more than you have.::

Lily offered Elhen a wan grin. "She ate the first two bowls."

::Good. I need her help.:: The queen turned her gaze to Oceana, who was perched on Lily's shoulder. ::You have given us a way to speak with those of our kind who are not here, and for that, we honor you. I wish for you to help me speak again to the one we felt across the water.::

Lily shuddered at the memory of the mysterious dragon's dark violence. "Why?" She'd be just fine never feeling that awfulness again.

She heard her dragon's pithy response saying exactly the same thing. Oceana didn't want to have anything to do with that kind of hate.

::Because I am queen,:: Elhen said quietly. ::His hate is mine to deal with.::

Kis stepped up beside her. ::And mine. We ask only that you carry our words, small blue-green friend.::

Lily could feel her dragon's hesitance. Play was one thing. This was something entirely different.

And it was maybe the reason that a small dragon who could talk through water had a cranky elf for kin. Because for all that Lily was short-tempered and strange, she knew what it was to be an orphan in your own clan—and she knew what it was to come to a new place and truly belong.

Belonging was everything.

And belonging had a price.

Lily lay down on her belly in the water and got nose-to-nose with her dragon. "The queen walked four days to come here to swim with you. So did Kis." Lily nodded her head at the dragons in the bay behind them. No longer playing. Standing guard. "They all hate water at least as much as you hate fire, and yet they spent the whole day letting you splash them and jump on their heads."

Oceana's eyes were big and tremulous.

Lily took in a breath, feeling the weight of the silence and of the words she had yet to speak. "They did that for you and for me, so we can feel like we belong. But everyone who belongs also has work to do. Whatever work they can, with whatever skills they have." The most basic rule of life in the kin village had never had deeper meaning. "We play, and we do things to help. Both matter. Both are part of how we belong."

Her dragon sighed, a small, sad sound that punctured Lily's chest. Then Oceana swam over, rested her chin on Lily's knee, and swished her tail in the water.

She would help.

-oOo-

It was not a battle cry—but it was a call nonetheless. One that Lovissa recognized. A queen.

She moved forward into the water, drawn by the impossible.

::I bid you welcome.::

Through the buzzing terror, Lovissa somehow managed to follow the words to the speaker. A white dragon, almost ghostly, stood at the water's edge, looking straight out as if she could see Lovissa and Baraken from her shore that looked nothing like this one.

Somehow, Lovissa managed to find the strength to speak. ::I cannot see you clearly. I can feel you well and see the shape of you dimly. But you are queen, as I am.::

::Yes. I am called Elhen.::

A queen whose name she knew. Lovissa forgot all thoughts of cold and fear. ::I speak to a queen who will come.:: It was not a question. Even as she spoke, her sense of certainty hardened. ::I am Lovissa. Do you know this name?::

Astonishment—and great joy. ::You are the grandmother of my grandmother, five times five.::

Lovissa could feel burbling merriment rising up her throat. ::I do not permit anyone to call me old, true though it may be.::

::As am I.:: The blurred white shape moved her head from side to side. ::You sent us the stars. To tell us where you are.::

Lovissa's legs trembled. This was no dream, no vision. The water felt far too real.

::Do not fear.:: The voice of the queen on the other side of the water gentled. ::I mean you no harm.::

Lovissa snorted, the words chasing some of her fear away. ::I speak to the ashes of queens past, and I have always believed they are quite capable of harm if I choose foolishly. Surely a ghost queen of the time to come could do the same.::

She felt surprise through the water. Awe, almost. ::You can speak to the queens who have come before?::

Lovissa felt the raw yearning from across the water—and felt the response rising from deep inside her, from the place that had always known she would be queen. She opened, sharing the memory of each who rose from the ashes, starting with Temar. Felt the mind on the other side of the water open in return.

Two old and tired queens, honoring those who had come before.

When the parade of queens of memory ended, there was silence. Stillness. And then a shaken, indrawn breath. ::We have forgotten much. There are no ashes here.::

The loss of such a thing nearly knocked Lovissa flat. Only Baraken's strong shoulder held her up. These dragons who would come were so very lost. She was not certain the survival of dragonkind was worth such a cost. ::You have no ashes. You befriend elves.::

::We do.:: The other voice took on an edge.

Lovissa held her head higher. This much she needed to do for herself, and for the warrior standing bravely at her side. ::I have lost many of my finest warriors to elf arrows and elf treachery. You may not share our hatred, but you will not disrespect it.::

A long pause. ::We do not know enough of the wars of your time. Many things are different, then to now. But I also see what has not changed.::

Lovissa could see no such things. She wanted, so very much, to back away from the water and push such horrors out of her knowing. ::I do not see what you see.::

::Then I will share my eyes.:: Elhen's voice pressed forward,

inexorable. ::*I see two queens, each seeking what is best for those they rule. Two queens of age and wisdom who know well what it means to embrace what will serve and resist what will harm.*::

The spiraling horror in Lovissa's chest somehow started to wind down. ::*I also see two such queens.*::

A small nod. ::*And I see two warriors, brave and true, who led us to the water.*::

Baraken snorted, but it wasn't fear emanating from him now. It was vast curiosity.

Lovissa watched as the yellow-gold dragon of her dreams stepped up to stand beside his queen. Even dripping wet and favoring a wing with old, scarred injuries that would have killed any dragon of her knowing, he was magnificent. His head dipped down nearly to the water. A bow of honor. Lovissa wasn't sure if it was meant for her or the immense black dragon at her side.

::*I am called Kis.*:: The rumble deepened, and a short, broad elf stepped up to his side. ::*And this is Irin. We are kin.*::

Lovissa could feel Baraken's war cry struggling to break free. She stood firm beside him, not sure whether to aid the loosening of the cry or its containment.

::*Speak.*:: The ghost-white queen spoke softly, but with a sternness Lovissa admired. ::*Words can do no harm, and they may help us to learn.*::

The ideas carried in words could lose the spring campaigns before they had even begun. Lovissa wondered what it would be like to live in a time when words were shared without fear. She struggled to find ones she could share in return. ::*We thought perhaps it was only your young and foolish who took elves for kin.*::

The elf at Kis's side tipped back his head and let a loud sound *ring up into the sky. ::Well, that might have described us once upon a time, old man.::*

Lovissa frowned, not sure whether she had offended.

The yellow dragon snorted and looked Lovissa squarely in the eyes. ::Some of our wisest and fiercest dragons also choose kin. We do not see it as a weakness. I am alive because this elf kept me so.::

Lovissa had seen his wing. It had perhaps not been a kindness, but she would not speak such thoughts into the water. She pointed her mind to the ghost queen instead. ::You have no elf.::

::I do not. But the queen before me did.::

Lovissa could not stop her indrawn hiss. ::She was weak, then.::

::No.:: A single word, quiet, but unbending. ::She was the most revered queen of our time.::

It was well done to speak thusly of one who had come before. Lovissa searched for words to honor such wisdom. The vision of the other bay wavered, grew dim.

::I am so sorry, small blue-green one.:: The ghost queen spoke crisply to someone Lovissa couldn't see. ::The dragon who permits us to see and hear and feel you grows weary. We must take a break.::

The second chosen of the Dragon Star. Lovissa's heart softened for the small one doing such large work. ::Will she recover?::

::I expect so.:: The queen spoke with the dry humor of one who was not overly concerned. ::I have seen her eat. We will fill her belly and return to you when we can. Before the sun falls out of the sky.::

That was half a day or more yet. Even Baraken could not stand in the cold, evil water that long. ::We must also eat. We will return.:: She did not say when. No dragon of her time would ever make such intentions known.

Especially when there were elves watching.

The white queen's head dipped. ::Until then, may the skies greet you kindly.::

Lovissa closed her eyes as the vision faded. The familiar words of departure spoken in her time had survived. Perhaps other things worth saving had also. But she wasn't yet sure she believed it, and the warrior beside her shook like one who had just lost all sense of what he might be fighting for.

Which meant that words had done more damage than all the spring campaigns of her lifetime.

CHAPTER 21

Lily's head hurt, but she knew this was a conversation that deeply mattered. She sat with as much patience as she could muster, her dragon on her lap, Alonia and Kellen tempting Oceana with the choicest nibbles from everyone's plates.

Attention and food her dragon was lapping up eagerly.

Lily, on the other hand, wanted to hide in a dark room and never see anyone ever again. Exhaustion of the fiercest kind had settled into her bones. She shook her head and tried to focus.

Elhen nodded at Kis. ::Are you certain that is where we should begin?.::

The old yellow dragon rumbled, sticking his head in a large bowl of stew. ::They are as stubborn as we are and entrenched in a fierce war. A dragon can only be moved so far in a single conversation, and the small one tires. We must be quick.::

The queen's concerned glance eased as she took in

Oceana's eager, lapping tongue. ::I believe the small one is the least of our worries.::

Kis licked the edges of his own bowl. ::Battles or not, their intense hatred of the elves must stop. They must begin that journey.::

Elhen dipped her head. ::I do not disagree. But as we found with the small one, it is perhaps easier if the first step we ask is one not quite so difficult.::

Irin snorted. ::You can't coddle battle-hardened dragons. They won't have it.::

::Indeed.:: The queen gave Kis a look that suggested history Lily didn't know. Difficult, honored history. ::I believe this is your conversation to have, old man. Lovissa is perhaps open to the idea that the elves must one day be seen as other than enemies. The warrior at her side has no such cracks in his hatred.::

Kis looked at his empty bowl for a long moment. ::I go where my queen tells me to go, but I don't know that this is my battle to fight.::

Irin's eyes narrowed. "Your gut talking to you again, old man?"

The old yellow dragon said nothing. He just looked at his kin.

Irin nodded once and rubbed a golden nose. "If he says it isn't his to do, I believe him. That gut of his kept us alive more times than I can count."

Elhen's head tipped. ::If not him, then who?::

It was a good question—and Lily was astonished to discover that somewhere under her blanket of weariness, she knew the answer. It flowed from deep inside her, rising like the tides. She knew exactly who could convince

Baraken and Lovissa to listen and maybe even to start to believe. She stroked her dragon's head spines. "Stay right here. I need to go talk to a dragon."

Heads turned toward her, some curious, some puzzled, but she didn't stop to explain, because she finally knew why she was still here and awake and hungry, and maybe even why she had a mark on her forehead. Oceana could help the dragons see and hear each other, but too many on both sides were scared and cranky and seeing things they didn't want to be true. Lily felt her lips twitching as she marched through the shallows. There was finally a use for her short temper and the fact that her skin still itched every time a dragon blew fire and the number of times she'd sat by Kis and tried to convince him to eat his breakfast.

She knew, better than anyone, how to deal with inflexible and cranky.

Kellen used kindness and gentle coaxing. Lily never had. That wasn't who she was. She was an elf who said exactly what she thought, even when it wasn't appreciated. And this was about to be her finest moment. She stomped over to where Afran stood, bone dry except for the wet sand sticking to his claws. "You're the one. You need to talk to them."

She'd never seen him look startled, but he looked that way now. ::Kis and Elhen know all that I would say.::

Probably because he'd been whispering it into their minds, but that didn't matter. "It's not what they say that will matter. It's who is saying it."

The huge dragon brought his head down and gazed straight into her eyes. ::I'm listening.::

She was about to insult him worse than Kellen ever had. "They need to hear it from someone who hasn't faced their worst fear yet."

Beside Afran, Karis jerked like someone had just shot her with an arrow.

Lily frowned. There was suddenly a tension in the air she didn't understand at all.

Afran blew out air, very softly. ::Explain.::

She swallowed, feeling every bit of the four days of dusty trails on her throat. "Those dragons across the water —they're really brave and they know how to fight, and they're smart. But they're scared because their future is different than what they thought it would be." Her chest squeezed. "They're standing on the shore, just like you. Their most scary thing hasn't happened yet, but they can see it, just like you can see the water. They haven't gotten in yet, just like you, and that means you understand them in a way that nobody else does."

Karis laid a hand, ever so gently, on her giant dragon's shoulder. "You're saying that Kis and Elhen aren't the right speakers for this message because they have faced their worst fear and gone through it."

The part of Lily that thought things and had learned not to say them out loud because they sounded too mean jerked on her throat. "Yes. Kis did that long before today." It was why he had been the first one in the water. A thousand waterfalls had nothing on falling from the sky.

Karis nodded. "Elhen too. She nears death."

Lily hadn't even thought of what the old queen must fear. She squeezed her eyes shut.

Afran blew gently on her face. ::You believe the

message must come from one of us who can yet see our greatest fear looming.::

Lily nodded slowly, the wild sadness that leaked off both Karis and Afran nearly knocking her to her knees. She didn't understand, but she could feel their pain. "I think the dragons of old need to hear from someone who hasn't gone in the water yet."

There were more words flooding out behind those ones, and they did push Lily to her knees. "One day, maybe Sapphire and Lotus will need to fly really far to bring the dragons of old to their new home."

Karis nodded—it was one of the ideas that had been much discussed through the winter.

Lily could feel relief and certainty rising inside her like a flood. "I don't think Oceana and I will go. We'll stay here with the ones like Kis and Elhen who can't go. It's not just five of us who will do the saving. It's everyone."

Afran's eyes glowed. ::You and your dragon will join us all together.::

Lily nodded, feeling lightheaded as the last piece fell into place. "Everyone's strength matters. But a great warrior knows when to use their strength."

She heard Kis snort behind her, but she kept her attention on Afran. "Kis got us here. Fendellen got the fliers in the water. Now it's your turn." She included Karis in her gaze. "Both of you, I think."

Karis raised an eyebrow. "Why?"

"I think you'll eventually be the ones who teach the old dragons." Lily blew out a breath. "They won't listen to me, or to Sapphire, or to our dragons. Fendellen, maybe, but she'll probably be too busy doing something dangerous."

Irin chuckled behind her. "You've always seen things clearly, missy."

Karis raised her eyebrows at the weapons master. "You think she's right?"

"I don't have a better idea."

Lily rolled her eyes. Irin never told anyone they were right. He always said they needed to sort things out for themselves, and preferably before somebody ran them through with a sword.

She felt very much like she had just done her sorting.

"They're back." Fendellen waded into the shallows and shook, spraying water everywhere. "I think the big warrior on the other side is going to start reciting recipes for elf stew soon, so if you've got something to say, you need to do it now."

Alarmed, Lily stepped back into the water, and into the hot soup of emotions seeping out of dragons near and far. She could feel the heat of hate from the big, black warrior at the center and a steady, solid wall keeping that heat under control.

::The queen's work,:: Fendellen said quietly. ::But Elhen tires.::

Suddenly Lily understood why there were so many dragons back in the water. So many large, fierce creatures who no longer looked remotely playful. Fendellen nodded at Afran. ::You try to talk with him. If he tries anything foolish, he answers to me.::

Lily gulped and squeezed forward, Oceana wrapped in her arms.

Afran loomed beside her, in the water before anyone had even noticed.

Except for a small, hissing blue-green dragon.

Lily eyed the head sticking up out of her arms. "Now isn't the time to be difficult."

Oceana glared at the big dragon who had never earned her trust.

They had no time for this. Lily turned a blue-green head by the chin until all her dragon could see was the eyes of her kin. "You won't like every dragon in the village or every dragon way out there in the water, just like Kis and Irin probably didn't like everyone they fought to keep safe. Maybe Afran will be your friend one day and maybe he won't, but it doesn't matter. This is who we belong to, and this is our part to do."

Oceana sniffed, but she turned her head back to the great charcoal gray dragon and edged her tail in his direction.

Afran nodded his head solemnly. ::I thank you.::

Lily managed not to roll her eyes as her dragon preened a little.

The large dragon stepped deeper into the water, his eyes on the enormous black warrior they could all see. The one breathing fire, his eyes full of hate. The one with daggers in his eyes for every elf on the back of a dragon.

Lily gulped. The dragons with kin were all standing in the front row. No coddling indeed.

It was Kis who spoke first, rumbling from Afran's side. ::One day, you will no longer fight the elves. If you are to survive, you will also need to stop hating them.::

::Never.:: The thought blasted across the water, crashing into Lily's head like a weapon.

::Enough.:: Afran's voice was as stern as Lily had ever

heard it. ::You must show respect. Kis is the finest warrior I have ever known. He gave all that he was to the battlefield. He does not ask anyone to stop fighting lightly.::

Lily would have done anything Afran demanded in that tone. The dragon who was kin to Kis was not nearly so easily swayed. ::He permits an elf to stand at his side. No such puny creature is required for battle.::

Irin snorted. "Those puny creatures are fighting you to the death, or you would have no reason for such hate."

The big black warrior raised his head, fire in his eyes—and froze as his queen stepped forward. "You are correct. One elf is nothing more than a pest, but in numbers, they can quell even the fiercest dragon. Our hate is justified, but we do not lack in respect for our enemies. Baraken speaks words in the way that our young warriors need to hear. They would confuse respect with fear."

A silence, and Lily could feel the sharp edges in the water easing a little.

Afran slowly inclined his head and ducked his nose down nearly to the bay. ::Do the elves make your skin crawl as much as this terrible water?::

A sound came out of Lovissa that sounded very much like laughter. "At least one of you has some sense. It is exactly thus. Our skin wants to escape the water and the sight of the elves both."

Afran waited a long moment before he spoke again. ::Those are instincts rooted deep in your skins and hearts. They will take a long time to change.::

Baraken's fire was a fearsome thing. ::There is no need to change.::

Oceana quivered—and then she thrashed her tail on the water's surface and blasted water.

Straight into Baraken's face.

Every dragon and every elf on both sides of the water froze. Lily felt like she might never breathe again as the fiercest warrior she had ever seen prepared to attack.

And then Kis rumbled his amusement loudly enough for the stars to hear. He craned his head down to Oceana and blew smoke at her head. ::I didn't know you could do that, small one.::

::Apparently, we aren't the only ones who sometimes underestimate those who are puny.::

Lily looked up to figure out who had spoken and gaped at the queen across the water.

Lovissa inclined her head. ::Respect, little one. We will think on what you have said.::

Lily figured she couldn't make anything worse than what her dragon had just done. "Think hard. The Dragon Star picked me to try to help save you, and I'm not going to be much use if you still want to make me into a stew."

Baraken's roar cut off sharply when Oceana lifted her tail.

Lovissa switched her gaze back to Afran. ::Are elves always so rude?::

Afran's voice remained steady and calm, but Lily was quite sure his eyes looked amused. ::I believe that is something you will have to judge for yourselves.::

Karis stepped out of the shadows of his side. "We invite you to know us. Slowly. At times of your choosing."

The queen's eye ridges slid up slowly. ::I will not

weaken my warriors. We must win the spring campaigns or there will be no dragonkind for you to save.::

Afran looked around at the collected dragons and shivering elves, and no one in the bay or across the water missed his rumbled reply. ::In that case, I suggest you start with swimming lessons.::

EPILOGUE

*L*ovissa watched the three young warriors standing on the edge of the sea, looking at Baraken like he'd asked them to compose cyclic ballads in elvish, and contemplated just how strange her elder years had gotten.

Swimming lessons.

They had chosen the bravest for this small beginning. Told them that fear gave their enemies openings in battle. That part had been Baraken's idea. A way to begin the slow process of changing their ways without weakening their warriors.

She would discuss this with the dragons over the waters at their next meeting. Change must be slow. Dragonkind must survive long enough to be saved.

But she already had seen changes, even though her finest warrior had told no one of the elves. He fought as fiercely as he ever had, but late at night, at the fires of victory, he spoke of small things he had noticed about the puny warriors they fought. Mostly weaknesses, but also things that made them real. That made them individuals. Some even worthy of respect.

A word here, a word there. Dripping like the infernal water.

Lovissa shuddered. When the Dragon Star once again reached its highest point in the sky, she would return to the sea. This they had agreed to with the dragons across the waters.

One of the young warriors working with Baraken managed to dip a claw into the water and jumped back, squealing like a dragonet and looking like she'd just sucked on a washberry. Lovissa waited until the student had her reaction back under control and then nodded. Offering the approval of a queen.

The young warrior preened. The other two looked abashed and edged closer to the water, learning to face what they feared most. One day, perhaps they would use that lesson to befriend their enemy and save everything that mattered.

Or perhaps she would reign over the time of swimming lessons. There were certainly stranger things queens had been known for.

Lovissa arched her neck and welcomed the warm rays from overhead. There was no hurry. For now, her dragons would put claws and tails in the water and begin to learn of bravery and fear and confronting unchangeable truths and permitting them to change.

She unsheathed her wings and waited for Baraken and his students to notice. It was time for her warriors to remember why she was queen. Always, she had led them into battle. Today, all that was required was that she wet a claw and offer a few words of encouragement. Tomorrow, perhaps they would work on tails. They had time. There were three more yet for the Dragon Star to choose.

Lovissa tossed herself off the cliff and began the steep glide down to the sea. Three more to be chosen. If they were anything like the first two, the shaking of all she held dear and true had only begun.

THANK YOU

We appreciate you reading!

As you might have guessed, there are more Dragon Kin books on the way. T The next one features an elf who dreams of boys and dragons, and at least one of those might come true. To hear about the next release, head to audreyfayewrites.com and sign up for the *New Releases* email list.

If you're a reader who likes to graze widely, you might enjoy some of Audrey's other books while you wait. There's everything from spacefaring singers to assassins and mermaids.

Shae & Audrey

Printed in Poland
by Amazon Fulfillment
Poland Sp. z o.o., Wrocław